FEAST OF THE SCORPION

James Pattinson

CHIVERS

THORNDIKE

This Large Print book is published by BBC Audiobooks Ltd, Bath, England and by Thorndike Press®, Waterville, Maine, USA.

Published in 2005 in the U.K. by arrangement with Robert Hale Ltd.
Published in 2005 in the U.S. by arrangement with Robert Hale Limited.

U.K. Hardcover ISBN 1–4056–3152–X (Chivers Large Print)
U.K. Softcover ISBN 1–4056–3153–8 (Camden Large Print)
U.S. Softcover ISBN 0–7862–7015–2 (Nightingale)

The text of this Large Print edition is unabridged.
Other aspects of the book may vary from the original edition.

Set in 16 pt. New Times Roman.

Printed in Great Britain on acid-free paper.

British Library Cataloguing in Publication Data available

Library of Congress Cataloging-in-Publication Data

Pattinson, James, 1915–.
    Feast of the scorpion / James Pattinson.
        p.   cm.
    ISBN 0–7862–7015–2 (lg. print : sc : alk. paper)
    1. Central America—Fiction. 2. Large type books. I. Title.
PR6066.A877F43 2005
823'.914—dc22   2004057988

CONTENTS

CHAPTER ONE

ROOM WITH A VIEW

Aston looked at his wrist-watch. 'Three hours to go. Just three hours.'

'Sure, Mark, sure,' McCall said. 'You don't have to tell us. We all know the time.'

He sounded edgy, which was strange for him. He walked to the window with that rangy, slightly rolling gait of his and stood there, gazing down into the street three storeys below and tugging at his gingery beard. He was six feet tall and all bone and sinew—bony face, bony shoulders, bony arms and legs—size eleven feet and hands made to the same scale.

The window was open but there seemed to be no air in the room. Aston glanced at Eduardo Vara and saw that he was sweating lightly—and that was unusual too. The sweat made his dark face shine like a polished boot. He was half Negro and so handsome he could have passed for an actor or a male model or even a gigolo; but he was none of these. His nose was straight and narrow with slightly flaring nostrils; there was near-perfection in the proportions of his face, and the curled black hair was bunched above it like a bush. Every movement that he made was as lithe and supple as a cat's, and with the same kind of

1

grace. Because of that amazing gracefulness he gave the impression of being smaller than he was; but looking at him closely you could see that he probably weighed nearer twelve stone than eleven. He carried the weight easily; it was no burden to him.

The fourth man in the room was the fleshy one; he was a roly-poly, a dumpling, amorphous. When he sat in a chair his body seemed to mould itself to the shape, filling all the available space like a jelly poured into a bowl. His name was Enrique Albores and he had one of those faces that can be gentle or sad or humorous, yet have about them a hint of ruthlessness too, as though hidden beneath the soft and mobile surface might be found a seam of iron.

They were all young. McCall, the oldest, was twenty-six, and he had fought in Vietnam. It was the United States Army that had taught him to handle a gun, and he had learnt his lesson well. But he was not shooting for them any more; he was enlisted in a different cause, in a different country. Like Vara, like Albores, he had a mission.

Aston was the odd man out: he had no mission; he had been drawn into the affair against his will, against his better judgement; as McCall might have said, it was not really his scene. But he was in it now and he had to go through with it, because it was too late to back out. He did not like it; there was not one

2

smallest piece of it that he liked; the whole idea of it repelled him, and he knew in his heart that it must end in disaster; he had the feeling in his bones. And yet he had allowed himself to be persuaded; against every argument of sanity he had allowed himself to become involved in a project from which only a few weeks ago he would have recoiled in horror. He still hated it; and yet he was now a part of it, was helping to set up an operation which appalled and terrified him. And why? For one reason only: Juanita.

He could hear the girl now—Juanita Merengo; the apartment had thin internal walls. He could hear the shower running and could hear her humming that tune again; always that tune. As he listened to those two muted sounds—the running of the shower and the pleasant humming of the tune—the picture of the girl was in his mind; that perfect body with the water glistening on the silken skin; the young, firm breasts and the enchanting curve of throat and chin and mouth; the dark, lustrous eyes and raven hair. What fatal chance had caused his path to cross with hers? Yet no chance really, for it had been planned as carefully as a military operation; and everything had gone according to that plan—Albores's plan, McCall's plan, Vara's, Juanita's.

And he had been the sucker.

McCall drifted away from the window.

Albores, slumped in a chair, lit a cigarette and blew smoke from his mouth and nostrils, as though a small bonfire had been set going inside him.

'That tune,' Vara said. 'Why does she always sing that tune?'

It was 'Greensleeves'. Aston had taught it to her, fingering the notes out of an old guitar he had picked up in a little junk shop down by the waterfront. Maybe a sailor had once owned the guitar and had sold it to raise money for a bottle of mescal or a girl or a poker stake. Who could tell? *Quién sabe?* as they would have said in Mendoza, giving that expressive lift of the shoulders which no Anglo-Saxon could reproduce to perfection. And what difference did it make?

'It is a good tune,' Albores said. 'Ask Mark. It comes from his country.' He sounded faintly amused, a smile lurking at the corners of his half-closed eyes.

'A good tune!' Vara seemed almost angry at the idea. 'It is nothing. Nothing at all. Worthless.'

'You have no ear for music, Eduardo.'

But it was not that, Aston thought. Vara's impatience with the tune sprang from other roots; it had to do with Juanita and him and the relationship between them. It had to do with Vara's feelings for the girl. It had to do perhaps with jealousy.

The room was not large, but it had always

been large enough for Aston; it had suited him well enough during the year and a half that he had been working in Mendoza. The furniture was not luxurious and it had taken a bit of a beating from earlier tenants, but he was not proposing to spend his life with it; he was only in Central America for a limited period, after which he would return to England. At least, that had been the programme mapped out before he had got himself mixed up in this thing. Now the future looked uncertain; there was no telling what might happen.

There were two other rooms opening off this one—the bedroom with its adjoining bathroom, from which could be heard the sounds of the girl under the shower, and a small kitchen. The house had been quite a classy residence in its time, but its best years were in the past and it had rather gone to seed; it could have used a coat or two of paint and some repairs here and there. Sometimes the tenants complained about faults in the plumbing and decaying window frames, but very little ever got done; and nobody liked to make too much fuss because there was a housing shortage in Mendoza and there were plenty of people only too ready to snap up the tenancies if they became available.

Another reason why nobody complained too loudly was that it was generally believed that certain high-ranking members of the administration were in the habit of skimming

5

some of the cream off the rents, and anyone who went around saying that these rents were extortionate and that something ought to be done about the drains or the rotting staircases or the crumbling brickwork was likely to get himself nothing more welcome than a visit from the police and possibly some trumped-up charge of disorderly behaviour in a public place or incitement to commit a crime against the State. And when it came to a question of crimes against the State the field of choice had virtually no limits.

Albores was blowing smoke rings. He was the only one who seemed to be entirely at ease; perhaps it was all that flesh on his bones that insulated him from nervous tension. And there was certainly nervous tension in the close air of the apartment. Aston could feel it. McCall and Vara were affected by it too, much as they might try to conceal the fact. Only Albores seemed immune.

And there were three hours still to go.

McCall was moving around like an animal in a cage; a wolf maybe.

'Why don't you keep still, Red?' Vara said. 'Do you have to do all that pacing up and down? If you want to walk why don't you go and walk in the street?'

McCall came to a halt in front of Vara. 'Does it bother you, Eddie?'

Aston wondered why he had to use that contraction of the name; he knew Vara hated

6

being called Eddie. Perhaps it was a way of getting some of the tension out of his system, to bait the other man.

'Yes,' Vara said, 'it bothers me.'

'Well, that's just too bad, isn't it, Eddie old pal?'

'Don't call me that,' Vara said.

'Why not? It's your name, isn't it?'

'It is not my name. You know very well it is not my name.'

'It's what I call you, pal.'

'And I am asking you not to call me that.'

'Asking?'

'I am telling you.'

'So what happens if I forget and still go on calling you Eddie, Eddie old pal?'

McCall was openly taunting him, and it seemed a foolish thing to do at such a time. There was no advantage to any of them in making Vara angry. More than anything else they needed to keep cool, to avoid bickering.

Vara seemed about to rise from his chair and there was an angry glitter in his eye. It looked like a fight boiling up, and a fight amongst themselves would be plain crazy. But Albores put a stop to that, easily, without even raising his voice.

'No,' he said. 'No, Eduardo.'

Vara subsided. Albores had authority; he had that indefinable something that made people obey him. He looked at McCall.

'And you stop needling him. What's gotten

7

into you? Do you want to sabotage the operation? Don't you think there are more important things than snapping at one another, for God's sake?'

McCall shrugged. 'Okay, I'll keep my mouth shut.'

'And don't call him that.'

'Are you telling me?'

'I am asking you.'

McCall grinned suddenly. 'Okay, I'll try to remember.' He turned the grin on Vara. 'Okay with you, Eduardo?'

Vara did not grin in return, but the glitter had faded from his eye. 'Okay with me, Red.'

'Maybe I should object to being called Red,' McCall said.

Albores blew smoke from his mouth. 'Do you?'

'No,' McCall said, 'I guess not.'

Aston could feel the tension ease. There was no sound from the bathroom now; the girl had stopped humming 'Greensleeves' and the shower had been turned off. He walked to the window and looked down on the Avenida Almirante Diaz, on the traffic moving along the wide thoroughfare. The avenue ran straight in each direction and most of the buildings lining it on either side were a trifle old, a trifle shabby, like the one in which Aston had his apartment. But about a hundred yards away on his left a new block was going up, a glass and concrete box which was destined to

8

accommodate government offices and provide one more source of grievance for the poor and homeless of the city. For such projects there was always money; for low price housing there was never enough.

From the window it was possible to see for a distance of perhaps two or three hundred yards up and down the Avenida Almirante Diaz and there was nothing to block the line of sight. Albores and the others had realised this from the start; it was the reason why they had been so interested in the room. They had been searching for a room and they had found it there. Aston might have wished that they had never taken an interest in his room had it not been for the fact that then he might never have met Juanita. She had brought trouble certainly, but he knew that, given the choice of trouble and Juanita or no trouble and no Juanita, he would still take the girl. Without her life would become empty and meaningless.

He heard a door behind him open and he turned away from the window as the girl came out of the bedroom. She was wrapped in a white towelling bathrobe that belonged to him and was too big for her, and her feet were bare. The men were all looking at her, but she was not embarrassed; she had a cool self-assurance and she was undoubtedly beautiful. If she had been less splendidly endowed in that respect she might not have been able to play so successfully the part for which she had been

9

cast. And then Aston would have been spared a world of trouble—and a world of sheer delight as well.

She said: 'The shower isn't working properly; there seems to be a blockage or something.' Her voice had a rich velvety quality.

'I know,' Aston said. 'Sometimes it goes like that.'

Her black hair had been swept carelessly back over her ears and there was an uneven fringe across her forehead. Her eyes were dark and lustrous; they seemed to glow, as if with a slow, smouldering fire. It was the eyes that had first drawn Aston to her with an immediate irresistible attraction, as though there had been in them some strange magnetism.

'You should have it seen to, Mark.'

He smiled, a trifle ruefully. 'There would hardly be much point in bothering about that—now.'

'No,' she said, 'there wouldn't, would there? Not now.'

Albores pursed his lips. 'I think you had better get dressed, Juanita.'

'There is time,' she said. 'There is plenty of time.'

'Nevertheless—'

Aston could see that Albores did not like her to be there dressed only in a bathrobe; perhaps he feared it might have an unsettling effect—especially on Vara. Not that the robe

10

revealed much; it was simply that they were all aware that she had nothing on beneath it, that the cord had only to come loose and her nakedness would be exposed. And perhaps to Vara the very fact that she should be wearing next to her skin a garment belonging to the Englishman was galling, suggesting as it did an intimacy that was distasteful to him. Yet he had no good cause for complaint on that score; it had been part of the plan and he must have agreed to it in the first instance. Perhaps he now regretted having done so. It was a little late for regrets.

'It's hot,' McCall said. 'You have anything to drink, Mark?'

'There's canned beer in the refrigerator. Do you want some?'

'I could use a beer.'

'How about you, Enrique?'

'Why don't we eat now?' Albores said. 'It could be quite a time before we get another meal.'

'If you like. It'll just be sandwiches. We're not frying today.'

Nobody smiled. It was not much of a joke.

'Sandwiches will be fine.'

'I'll make them,' Juanita said.

She went into the kitchen, her bare feet soundless on the worn carpet. Aston followed her and closed the door.

'What do we use for sandwiches?' she asked.

11

'I could open a tin of Spam. And there are some tomatoes. Mustard if you want it.'

'Let's settle for Spam and tomato. Are you hungry?'

'Not really.'

'You're too tensed up.'

'You can bet your life I am. I'm not used to this, you know. It's all pretty new to me. Maybe you've been through it before.'

She shook her head, making the hair swing. 'No, Mark, never before. It's the first time for me too.'

'And maybe the last. Maybe the last for all of us.'

'Don't worry, Mark. It will be all right.'

'I hope so. God, I just hope so. But I'm not counting on it.'

He found the tin of Spam and opened it. He pulled the door of the refrigerator open and took out the tomatoes and some cans of beer. Juanita began to cut the bread, but the loose sleeves of the bathrobe kept getting in the way. She put the knife down and rolled them up over her elbows, then started again. Aston took some glasses from a cupboard and began opening the cans and pouring out the beer.

The kitchen was small and it was hotter in there than in the other room. Yet the girl still looked cool. She had a fresh, clean odour of scented soap about her that Aston found intoxicating. There was a kind of enchantment in her movements even as she cut the

12

sandwiches, in the smooth curve of her shoulder where the robe had fallen away, in the gleaming clusters of her hair. Watching her he forgot what he was doing and allowed some of the beer to froth over the top of the glass. He put down the glass and the can, moved up behind her and pressed his lips into the warm hollow between her neck and shoulder.

'No,' she said: 'It is not the time for that.'

'Any time is, Juanita.'

He put his hands on her arms and turned her so that she was facing him. The knife she had been using was still in her right hand and there was tomato juice on her fingers, but he cared nothing for that. When she was near him his pulse raced and he could not think normally. It was the reason why he had allowed himself to become involved in an affair in which he had no desire to be involved and why he had to go through with it to the end, whatever that end might be. For if he did not go through with it he would lose her, and losing her was the one thing he could not bear to contemplate.

'Juanita!' His voice was husky and he seemed to choke on the word. 'Oh, God, Juanita, why did it have to be like this?'

CHAPTER TWO

MEETING

It began at a football match. Atletico Mendoza were playing San Sebastian at the Colon Stadium in a match that might well decide the Championship and the ground was packed to capacity. It was a public holiday and Mendoza was football mad. Football was a game that could even make people forget their troubles—poverty, hunger, oppression; it was a kind of drug, but it could rouse strong passions. For that reason there was a stout wire fence all round the playing area at the Stadium and the players reached it by way of a concrete tunnel.

An important match could easily spark off riots in the city, especially if Atletico should have the misfortune to lose, and extra police were always on duty to deal with trouble on such occasions. But it was when Atletico came up against Cresta, the other big Mendoza club, that the worst excesses were likely to occur, and then the Army might have to be called out to deal with the situation.

Aston should have gone to the Atletico-San Sebastian match in the company of another employee of the Anglo Insurance Company, a man named Peters. Peters was older than

14

Aston and was deputy manager of the Mendoza office. He had married a local girl and had a house in the suburbs; he liked it in Mendoza and had no desire to return to England. Aston was well aware Peters hoped, and indeed expected, to step into the manager's shoes when that gentleman retired, which was likely to be in a few years' time; he was the cautious type, very hard-working and careful never to put a foot wrong, so he would probably make it. Aston had a feeling that it was because Peters feared there might be trouble at the match that he had called off at the last moment, although he had given another reason.

'I'm sorry to let you down, Mark, but these domestic crises have a way of cropping up at the most inconvenient times.'

Peters had been vague about the precise nature of the domestic crisis that had demanded his presence at home rather than at the Colon Stadium. He was a tall, thin man with a long neck and a prominent Adam's apple. He wore gold-rimmed glasses and a small moustache that looked distressingly impoverished, and his eyes had the anxious look of a man who is always on the alert for the slightest hint of disaster and lives in constant expectation that it may at any moment creep up on him from behind and catch him unprepared.

'Don't let it bother you,' Aston said.

'You'll go nevertheless?'

'Oh, yes, I'll go. Why not?'

'It's never quite as enjoyable when you go alone.'

'Well, maybe I'll pick up a bird to keep me company.'

Peters appeared uncertain whether or not to take that as a serious suggestion. 'I think you should be careful what you do,' he said. 'Remember we are the representatives of Anglo Insurance in Mendoza and must always uphold its reputation.'

Aston laid on a finger along the side of his nose. 'You can trust me to behave with discretion.' He had difficulty in not laughing; Peters was so utterly serious. The reputation of Anglo Insurance indeed! As if anything he might do was likely to affect business one way or the other. But Peters seemed to regard the Anglo Insurance office in Mendoza as an oasis of civilised conduct in a desert of barbarism. Anything that might have tarnished the image of strict propriety presented by the Company would have distressed him almost as much as a personal disgrace.

'Never forget,' Peters said, 'that we are in a position of trust. It is by the manner in which we behave, whether working or relaxing, that the Company is judged.'

'I won't forget,' Aston said.

It was not a good match, and it ended in a draw, which settled nothing. Neither side had

16

scored a goal and the crowd probably felt cheated, but there had been nothing to rouse the worst passions. Nevertheless, it would have been little short of a miracle if there had been no violence after the game. With so many San Sebastian supporters in the streams of people spilling out from the exits some physical encounters between them and disgruntled Atletico fans were inevitable.

Aston had walked scarcely fifty yards from the Stadium when he saw a car with San Sebastian registration plates being attacked by a gang of youths. The car had been brought to a halt by the crush of people and the youths were rocking it violently from side to side in an apparent attempt to turn it over. There were four people inside—two men and two women. The men were shouting angrily and the women looked scared. Aston thought they had some reason to be, because some of the youths had produced knives, and one of them even had a fireman's axe and was starting to smash the windows with it. The others were still trying to turn the car over, but it was a big, heavy Chevrolet and they were not having much success in that line and Aston was wondering when the police would come along and put a stop to it.

Then the youth with the axe reached across the bonnet and smashed the windscreen, and that, as far as the driver was concerned, seemed to be the last straw. He hauled a

17

revolver from his pocket and shot the youth in the chest.

It all began to happen then. The women screamed; the youth dropped the axe and slid off the bonnet of the car; one of the other youths got the rear door open and grabbed one of the women; she scratched his face with her fingernails and he gave a yell, hooked his fingers in the neck of her dress and ripped it open down the front. By this time the driver had emptied his revolver and two more youths were lying on the ground with bullets in them. The others got at the driver with their knives and there was nothing at all light-hearted about the business any more; it was just brutal, vicious and bloody.

And then the police arrived on the scene and started adding a bit more brutality and viciousness.

Aston felt someone tugging at his sleeve. It was a girl, and he had an idea that he had seen her somewhere before, but for the moment he could not remember just where. She was the kind of girl he would have been glad to see anywhere and at any time.

'Please,' she said. 'Please help me.'

They were being jostled by the crowd. More police had arrived and they were driving people away from the car, shouting orders and wielding batons like drovers dealing with a herd of cattle. There was a hint of panic in the air; there could easily have been a stampede.

18

'I'm scared,' the girl said.

She looked scared, Aston thought; her eyes were wide and her voice trembled a little. He could understand her apprehension; it was an ugly situation and she appeared to be unaccompanied.

'Are you alone?'

'I was with some people but I lost them.' She gazed anxiously round, as though searching for her lost companions. 'I can't see them anywhere.'

'Don't worry,' Aston said. He was not at all sure that he wanted her to find them. 'Just stay close to me.'

He took her arm, guiding her through the crowd; frequently she was crushed against him by the pressure of human beings milling round them, and he felt a surge of excitement at the intimacy of that contact, as though a current of electricity had passed between them.

It took them fifteen minutes to get clear of the press, and in all that time they had spoken scarcely another word. They finally came to a halt at a tram stop.

'It was very kind of you to help.' She sounded breathless. 'I won't bother you any more.'

'It was no bother,' Aston said. 'And don't you think you should tell me your name?'

'Juanita—Juanita Merengo.'

'I'm Mark Aston.'

'You are American?'

'English. I thought the accent would have given me away.'

'You speak Spanish well. Are you on a visit to this country?'

'Not exactly. I work here.'

'Oh, so you will not be leaving?'

'Not for some time.'

He thought she seemed pleased about that, and he hoped she was. And now that he had met her he had no intention of letting her go— at least, not without a struggle.

'Why don't we go somewhere and have something to eat?' he suggested. 'Then you can tell me all about yourself.'

It was the first time he had seen her smile, and it was an enigmatic kind of smile. He had an uneasy feeling that secretly she might be laughing at him.

'Do you really want to know all about me?'

'Everything.'

'You don't realise what you're asking.'

'It doesn't matter.'

'I don't know whether I ought to accept such an invitation from a perfect stranger.'

'We're hardly strangers now. I came to your aid when you asked me, remember? Don't you think you owe me a little in return for that?'

He wondered just how many people had been killed or injured in that nasty piece of business with the Chevrolet, but he had no intention of going back to inquire. He would read about it in the papers.

'Perhaps you are right,' she said. 'I do owe you something. You've been very kind.'

'It's settled then?'

'It's settled.'

A tram drew up at the stop. They got in. They were jammed together by a crush of passengers and again the pressure of her body against his set his pulse racing.

'What about your friends?' he said.

'What about them?'

'Won't they be worried at losing touch with you?'

'I don't think so. I'll ring them later perhaps.' She sounded unconcerned, and if she were not bothered, Aston thought, there was certainly no reason why he should be.

They had a meal in a café in the Calle Santiago, and it was not until it was almost finished that he remembered where he had seen her before.

'At the Colon Stadium. Of course.'

'What are you talking about?' she asked.

'I felt sure I recognised you. You were sitting not far away from me at the match.'

She wrinkled her nose. 'It's not very flattering, is it?'

'Not flattering?'

'That you should take so long to remember. I knew you at once.'

Aston stared at her in surprise. 'You mean to say you saw me there and that afterwards in all that crowd you recognised me?'

21

'But of course I did. That was why I asked you to help me. In a way it was as if we had already met. And I felt sure I could trust you. You have such a reliable sort of face.'

He was not sure whether to be pleased about that or not. 'Reliable! Is that how it strikes you?'

She turned on the enigmatic smile. 'You sound a little put out. Does it annoy you to have your face described as reliable?'

'It's had worse things said about it.'

'But perhaps you would have preferred me to say that I could not forget it because it is so handsome. Have I injured your masculine vanity?'

He could see the mischievous laughter in her eyes. She was teasing him but he did not mind.

'You really believe I am as vain as that?'

'All men are vain—if only they would admit it.'

'And not women?'

'Women are too, of course; that goes without saying.'

'Do you include yourself in that judgement?'

She answered only with a smile, but it occurred to him that if anyone had reason to be vain, she had. Yet she had none of the airs of vanity, and he would not have said that she was consciously making an effort to captivate him. But perhaps she did not need to.

'On second thoughts,' she said, examining him with a frank, unwavering gaze, 'perhaps one might admit that it is handsome—in a way.'

'What kind of way would that be?'

'The way an Epstein sculpture is perhaps. A little rugged, shall we say?'

Aston grinned. 'Let's cut the compliments. Tell me about yourself.'

'There is not much to tell. I am twenty-one years old. I studied botany at the University but didn't take a degree.'

'You mean you didn't complete the course?'

'That's so. You're looking at a drop-out.'

'You don't look like one.'

'What should a drop-out look like?'

'Well—' He had in his mind a stereotype picture of the breed—scruffy, dirty, tangle-haired, in patched jeans and faded shirt, barefooted maybe. The picture certainly did not match Juanita Merengo in any respect; there was nothing scruffy about her.

'You think I should look like a hippy?'

'I'm rather glad you don't. Does your family live in Mendoza?'

All the answer he got to that was a vague shake of the head. He had the impression that she did not wish to talk about her family.

'You work here?'

'Yes,' she said, 'I work here.' But she did not enlarge on the bare statement. She was not really telling him much.

23

'And you,' she said. 'Let's talk about you.'

He told her that he worked for the Anglo Insurance Company at their offices in the Calle Honduras and that he had an apartment on the Avenida Almirante Diaz. She listened with polite attention, but he had a feeling that she was not deeply interested. It was almost as though she had heard it all before. Which was ridiculous.

He paid the waiter and they went out on to the Calle Santiago. Night had fallen and the street-lamps were on and all the shop windows were lighted up; the neon signs over the cafés and night-clubs and cinemas were making a garish display and the pavements were crowded.

'Would you like me to take you home now?' Aston asked.

She glanced at him. 'Does that mean you want to get rid of me?'

Aston shook his head. 'That's the last thing I want. I merely thought you might have better things to do than tagging along with me.'

'I have one room,' she said, 'in a house full of similar rooms. That's my home in Mendoza. It doesn't have such a great attraction that I'd ever want to hurry back to it. But I don't wish to make a nuisance of myself.'

'You wouldn't even know how to begin.'

'Well, if you really do enjoy my company—'

'I do. Just at this moment I can't think of anything I would enjoy more.' He looked at

24

her and knew that it was the truth. 'It's going to be a wonderful evening,' he said. 'Just wonderful.'

*   *   *

It was past midnight when he left her at the house that was full of rooms. The lighting was rather poor and he could not see it very clearly, but at a rough guess he would have said it was quite a few steps lower down the ladder than the house on the Avenida Almirante Diaz where he had his own apartment. It was in a steep little street where all the houses seemed to be clinging together for mutual support; the walls were whitewashed stucco, but the plaster was cracked and falling away in places. All the windows had wooden shutters and there were small iron balconies attached to those on the upper floors, the kind beneath which young men with guitars traditionally stood and serenaded their ladies. As far as Aston could see at that moment there was no one doing any serenading, so possibly it was a dying industry; or maybe he had arrived too late.

'Mine is two floors up,' she said; but she did not invite him to walk up and take a look at it.

'When do I see you again?' he asked.

'Do you wish to see me again?'

'There'd have to be something badly wrong with me if I didn't.'

'Well,' she said, 'I see no reason why it couldn't be arranged, do you?'

'Tomorrow?'

'It is already tomorrow.'

'Today then.'

'Are you in so much of a hurry?'

'For me it can't be too soon.'

'Perhaps in the morning you will have changed your mind.'

'About that,' he said, 'I would never change my mind. But perhaps it's you who don't wish to see me.'

'If I must confess the truth,' she said, 'it would not displease me to see you again. It would not displease me at all.'

She was standing in the doorway and her face was in shadow, but he knew that the smile was there again, enigmatic, faintly teasing and utterly enchanting. He took half a pace forward and drew her to him, and she made no resistance but merely laughed softly, as though she had known it must be like this. He kissed her then for the first time and was unaware that the net had closed around him, the invisible net with its unbreakable mesh from which there would be no escape.

CHAPTER THREE

INTELLIGENT GIRL

'Did you go to the match?' Peters asked.

'Yes, I went.'

He had run into Peters in the doorway of the building on the corner of the Calle Honduras and the Avenida Berisso where the Anglo Insurance Company had its offices. Peters looked very dapper in a pale grey Trevira suit and a white nylon shirt. His gold-rimmed glasses were polished to a gleaming brightness and there was a lingering odour of aftershave lotion about him. 'A good game?'

'Lousy,' Aston said. 'Not a single goal.'

They walked to the lift.

'I believe,' Peters said, 'there was some trouble after the match. Three people killed and a number injured.'

'Yes. I saw it.'

Peters looked concerned. 'You were not involved, I hope.'

'No; I avoided that. You can put your mind at rest; the Company's name won't be dragged through any mud.'

They got into the lift with a couple of other men and three secretaries chattering away like agitated starlings.

27

Peters said, frowning slightly: 'It gets worse and worse—all this violence at football matches. We should never have taught them the game; they haven't got the temperament to play it in the right spirit.'

'From what I read in the English papers it doesn't seem as if there's an abundance of the right spirit knocking around in the Mother Country either.'

Peters had no answer for that one. They got out on the sixth floor.

'Did you have any—um—company at the match?'

'If you mean did I pick up a bird, the answer's no, I didn't.'

'Just as well perhaps.'

'But one picked me up.'

Peters looked startled. 'You're joking.'

'Not at all. She needed my help.'

'In what way, for goodness' sake?'

'She'd lost touch with her friends and needed a bodyguard, so she chose me for the job.'

'That sounds a pretty thin story. What kind of a person was she?'

'It transpired during the course of an interesting conversation that she was a drop-out.'

Peters looked worried. 'I hope you gave her the brush-off. I mean to say, you don't want to get mixed up with anyone of that type, do you?'

'You'd be surprised just how much I want to get mixed up with someone of that type. For your information, the encounter blossomed into a most enjoyable evening.'

Peters's worried expression deepened. 'Oh, dear! I don't care for the sound of that. I hope you know what you're doing.'

'Oh, yes,' Aston said; 'I know what I'm doing. I'm meeting her again this evening.'

*   *   *

Sometimes a second meeting could be a mistake; it could seem as though you were with a different girl, an indifferent substitute which had been slipped in in place of the original model. The enchantment of the first romantic encounter had a nasty way of evaporating during the night and you wondered what on earth had attracted you in the first place, because, whatever it was, it was certainly not there any longer.

But it was not like this with Juanita. Any doubts that might have been building up in Aston's mind were dispelled the instant he saw her; a single glance and he knew that here was the one girl for whom he might have searched all his life and never found but for that marvellous stroke of good fortune outside the Colon Stadium. Suppose, after Peters called off, he had decided not to go to the match. Then he would never have met her. It scarcely

29

bore thinking about. By what apparently small and insignificant decisions the entire course of a man's life could be switched on to a different track.

He called for her at the house with all the rooms, and it looked even dingier at a second viewing. There were some bits of washing hanging from some of the balconies and there were a few characters lounging about who really did look like hippies, or maybe worse. He wondered how a girl like her could bear to live in such a place; but maybe she was not earning a lot and had to go for the cheapest accommodation she could find.

He thought maybe she had been having some doubts about this second meeting too, but there was nothing in her manner to indicate that she had. She seemed really pleased to see him.

'So you didn't change your mind.'

'Did you think I would?'

'I thought you might.'

'Perhaps you hoped I would.'

'No, I didn't hope that.'

'So you're glad I came?'

'I'm glad,' she said.

It was even better than the first evening. Aston was happy and he believed the girl was too. Either she enjoyed his company or she was putting on a pretty convincing act; and he did not think it was an act; it was too spontaneous, too obviously genuine.

She knew Mendoza better than he did; she knew places to go to that he had never even heard of, places where young people congregated and ate and drank, listened to music and danced and talked. At one of these night-spots called The Weeping Crocodile, which was in a cellar under a bakery and was so hot even the floor was sweating, he intercepted a glance of recognition that passed between her and a group at a table in a corner.

'Friends of yours?' he asked.

She answered hurriedly: 'Just some people I know.'

There were three of them—men. One was lean, red-haired, with a beard; another was dark and plump; the third was coloured, handsome, with a kind of tense look about him.

Aston and the girl sat down at another table. There was a steel band working away on a small stage at one end of the room. The musicians were all black; they could have been imported from Trinidad.

'I could introduce you if you wish,' Juanita said.

'To those three? Why would I want to share you with them? I'm happy as we are.'

'I'm happy too,' she said.

'Truly? You're not just saying that to please me?'

'Truly, Mark.'

They danced to the music of the steel band.

Over the girl's shoulder Aston encountered the intense gaze of the coloured man; his eyes seemed to follow them, watching every movement. When they returned to their table that unwavering gaze was still on them.

'The dark one in the corner seems very interested in you,' he said.

'What makes you think that?'

'He watches you all the time.'

'And does it bother you?'

'It would bother me if you were with him instead of me. It would really bother me then.'

'Mark,' she said, 'I do believe you're becoming possessive.'

'Do you mind if I am?'

She thought it over for a few moments; then she said: 'No, I don't think so. It's rather a nice feeling to be wanted.'

It was a pretty nice feeling to want someone too. He began to imagine what it would be like to have her with him always; and he thought it would be just fine.

Possibly she had been thinking along roughly similar lines, for suddenly she asked: 'How long will you be staying in Mendoza? I mean it's not permanent, is it?'

'No, it's not permanent.'

'But you don't have to go back to England soon?'

'Oh, no; I've got another three or four years before that happens.'

It seemed to please her. 'I'm glad you're

going to be around for a while.'

'I'm glad too,' he said. 'And I'm glad you're glad.'

He looked past her and again encountered the burning gaze of the coloured man. He was not quite so glad about that.

*   *   *

Peters came up behind him in the entrance of the office building just as he was leaving. Peters took his arm in a confidential way and said:

'If you haven't already got something arranged for Tuesday evening, Mark, why don't you bring Miss Merengo to dinner? Eva and I would be very happy if you would.'

Peters had not met Juanita and Aston guessed that he was keen to see what she was like. A private little dinner party would provide the opportunity for a discreet inspection, from which he could decide whether or not Aston was making a fool of himself and likely to bring disgrace on the Company. Aston was not particularly attracted by the prospect of an evening with Peters; he would have preferred to have Juanita to himself; but Peters was his superior and it would not have been diplomatic to give a blunt refusal to the invitation. Besides, it might not be at all a bad idea to show Juanita to Peters; one evening in her company would surely put

33

at rest any qualms he might have concerning her. And though he didn't give a damn whether Peters approved or not, it would certainly be all to the good if he did.

'That's very good of you,' he said. 'I'll consult Juanita and if it's okay with her I'll be pleased to come.'

'Eva has been asking why I don't get you to drop in more often. She likes you, Mark. Did you know that?'

'I didn't, but it's very gratifying.'

'There seems to be something about you that women go for.'

'Now wait a minute,' Aston said.

'No seriously, I mean it,' Peters said; and he did indeed look serious. But that, of course, was the way he usually looked, life being to him a serious business and not at all a laughing matter. 'I don't know what it is. You're not exactly handsome, are you?'

'I've never imagined so.'

Peters gave him a thorough inspection, as though searching for that indefinable something which might be attractive to women; but apparently he failed to run it to earth, for he gave a baffled shake of the head and said: 'Well, I don't know what it is, I'm sure; but I'm not a woman, so perhaps I wouldn't. You're pretty husky of course, so maybe it's that.'

Aston wondered whether there was a hint of jealousy involved, but dismissed the idea.

34

Peters was not the type to be jealous; he was simply puzzled by something for which he could discover no rational explanation, and he was a man who liked a rational explanation for everything.

'Well,' Aston said, 'I'll let you know.'

'Let me know?'

'About the dinner.'

'Oh, that,' Peters said. 'Yes, do.'

*   *   *

When he mentioned it to Juanita she said yes, of course they must go. 'It would be impolite to refuse. And besides, I should love to meet your Mr. Peters.'

'He's not my Mr. Peters. I don't accept any responsibility for him. He belongs to the Company—body and soul.'

'And you don't?'

'As far as I'm concerned the Company is just something that pays me for a job of work.'

'No loyalty?'

'I don't see why anyone should be expected to show loyalty to a faceless thing like an insurance company.'

'Or to a country?'

'Well, a country is different, isn't it?'

'Yes,' she said with an oddly pensive expression, ' a country is different.'

'I'll accept the invitation then?'

'Yes, Mark, do that.'

35

It was a more enjoyable evening than Aston had anticipated. After some initial wariness Peters seemed to take to Juanita, and Aston was amused to see how his resistance melted in the warmth of her personality. With Eva there was simply no ice to break. She was a plump, dark-haired little woman, full of high spirits and infectious laughter and at least ten years younger than her husband. With no great pretensions to beauty, she had nevertheless undoubted charm; she put Aston in mind of a cuddly toy and was the last kind of person he would have imagined Peters being drawn to. Someone more dignified, more serious, more aware of the responsibilities of being the wife of the deputy manager of the Mendoza offices of the Anglo Insurance Company would have seemed a more likely choice. Similarly, he found it difficult to see what had induced her to marry a stick like Peters; but she seemed to be happy enough with him, so perhaps it was a case of the attraction of opposites.

The house was modern but not large; it was the kind you might have found on a surburban building estate in England. It was pleasantly furnished and had air-conditioning, which was a boon in that climate. Eva was an excellent cook and it was one of the best meals Aston had eaten in quite some time. Perhaps Peters had married her for her cooking.

Peters filled Juanita's wine-glass and got down to a bit of probing.

'Mark tells me you were at the University.'

'Yes.'

'But you left prematurely?' Peters spoke careful, correct Spanish. Both Juanita and Eva spoke fluent English but he would have considered it impolite to a guest not to use her native language.

'Yes,' she said. 'I decided that a degree was not necessary for the kind of work I intended doing.'

Peters raised his eyebrows at this. 'No? I should have thought a degree would have been a desirable qualification whatever you intended doing.'

She smiled at him. 'Do I detect a note of disapproval?'

He looked faintly disconcerted. 'It's hardly for me to approve or disapprove. The decision is yours, and you have made it. Nevertheless—'

'Nevertheless, you think I should not have dropped out?'

'I think there may well come a time when you will regret having done so.'

'That is possible,' she admitted. 'But there were reasons.'

Peters chewed a morsel of fricasseed chicken and swallowed it. Aston thought he might be going to ask her what the reasons were, but instead he said:

'Mark didn't tell me what kind of work it is that you do.'

She treated him to her enigmatic smile. 'He couldn't very well do that. I didn't tell him.'

It was evident to all of them that she had no intention of telling Peters either. He reddened slightly but did not pursue the subject.

'I think it was so romantic,' Eva said, 'the way you met Mark. Quite like a knight in shining armour galloping to the rescue.'

'Now,' Aston said, 'you really mustn't build it up into something big. There was practically no rescuing to do and there was never any great danger.'

'Perhaps there was some danger nevertheless,' Eva said, glancing from one to the other with a roguish eye. 'For both of you.'

'That kind of danger,' Aston said, 'I would go a long way to find.'

Eva laughed, but Peters appeared unamused. Aston wondered whether he was still worrying over the question of what Juanita did for a living; it was the sort of thing that would bother him.

When they had finished eating Eva went to the kitchen to make coffee. Juanita accompanied her and Peters ushered Aston into what he called the lounge. He offered cigars, but Aston refused.

'No, of course, you don't smoke, do you?'

'I've never felt the urge.'

Peters selected a cigar for himself and lit it

38

with great care, like a surgeon performing some delicate operation. 'I'm not entirely happy,' he said.

Aston glanced at him in surprise; it sounded as though Peters were about to confide some domestic trouble. Which would have been embarrassing. But it was not that; it was something of a broader nature about which he was not happy: the state of the country.

'There's all this unrest among the workers—left-wing stuff. Students too. It makes people uneasy; there's a feeling of insecurity all round.'

'If people feel insecure maybe they'll buy more insurance. Could be good for business.'

'It's no use selling more insurance if we're going to pay out heavily on claims; no profit in that. And with all these so-called urban guerrillas making a nuisance of themselves, no one is safe. No one of any importance, that is. Why, I might even be kidnapped myself.'

'For what purpose?'

Peters worked away at his cigar, puffing out smoke like a mouse in a lung cancer experiment. 'You know the pattern. They might demand a whopping great ransom from the Company; a handout to the poor of the city, that kind of thing. It's been done before.'

He had apparently been giving the subject a deal of thought, and the risk of kidnapping perhaps seemed very real to him. Possibly it was very real. Aston thought of suggesting that

39

he should take out some insurance to cover the risk, but decided that Peters would not be amused; to him it was no laughing matter.

'I suppose if it comes to that, I could be kidnapped too.'

'It's hardly likely,' Peters said. 'They go for rather more important victims.'

There was, apparently, a certain class distinction in the kidnapping business. Aston felt that he was being put in his place.

'Do you take any precautions?' he asked.

'I drive to the office by a different route each day. Apart from that, what can I do? If they really mean to get you, they will.' He took some more smoke out of the cigar and watched it drifting away. 'It's not so much myself I'm concerned about; but think what it would cost the Company if they had to pay out a ransom.'

Aston would have suspected Peters of joking if he had not known that the deputy manager never joked, particularly with regard to matters concerning the Company. So perhaps he feared they might hold it against him personally if he allowed himself to be kidnapped and thus made it necessary for them to fork out ransom money. It might even have a bad effect on his prospects of promotion.

Any further discussion of the subject was halted by the reappearance of Eva and Juanita with the coffee. For the rest of the evening they talked of a variety of things, but Peters made no more mention of his fears regarding kidnapping. And he failed to discover just what it was that Juanita Merengo did for a living.

*   *   *

'I like them,' Juanita said when they had left the house. 'Yes, I like them very much.'

'Even Peters?'

'Yes. He is a little stiff perhaps, but that is his way.'

'Yes, that is his way.'

'They are nice people. I think they are happy with each other. It is a pity that we—'

'Yes?' he said questioningly. 'Why don't you go on? What is a pity?'

She gave a slightly nervous laugh. 'Nothing. It was a thought that came into my head, but it is nothing.'

He saw that it was all the answer he was going to get, and he did not question her further. There were things she was keeping from him, he was aware of that; but perhaps one day she would take him completely into her confidence. He hoped that day would be soon. She seemed depressed when he kissed her goodnight; a little sad perhaps. He wondered what was on her mind but he went away without asking.

'She seems an intelligent girl,' Peters said; 'besides being extremely attractive. What I fail to understand is why she should have dropped out of university. She doesn't strike me as being the drop-out type. Would you say she was?'

It was the morning after the dinner party and they were waiting for the lift to take them up to the sixth floor.

'No,' Aston said, 'I wouldn't say that.'

'I mean it seems so irresponsible, and there again she doesn't give the impression of being an irresponsible person, does she?'

'No, she doesn't.'

'So what's the answer?'

'I don't know. Perhaps the course didn't appeal to her any more.'

'What was she reading?'

'Biology.'

'It's not a subject you'd expect a person to lose interest in.'

'Maybe something else came up that had a stronger pull.'

'Like what, for instance?'

'Well, a mission of some kind.'

'You think she has a mission?'

'I don't know.'

'I wish you'd find out, Mark. I wish you'd find out what kind of work she does. You see how she turned the question last night.

Frankly, I'm a shade bothered about it—on your account.'

They went up in the lift and got out on the sixth floor. The building was air-conditioned and gave an impression of being almost clinically hygienic; it was poles apart from that old decaying house with the iron balconies and wooden shutters in which Juanita lived. Perhaps this was the kind of thing she was rebelling against—this contrast between rich and poor. If she was rebelling.

'As a person,' he said, 'what do you think of her?'

Peters glanced at him quickly, as though surprised that he should ask such a question. 'Didn't I tell you? Oh, I like her, Mark; I like her a lot. Eva likes her too. Eva says she's one of the nicest persons she's ever met.'

'Well, good for Eva,' Aston said.

CHAPTER FOUR

SOME FRIENDS

A week later she had moved in with him at the apartment on the Avenida Almirante Diaz. It had come about so naturally, as though it had been inevitable from the first, that he could not be certain whether it had been her suggestion or his; it was a kind of tacit mutual

43

agreement, requiring no discussion. She did not give up her own room, and he suspected that she was keeping it as a possible way of retreat if things did not turn out well; not committing herself completely to the new arrangement until it had been fully tested.

Aston was content with this state of affairs—for the present. He was happier than he had ever been. When he looked back at what life had been before his meeting with Juanita it looked grey and dreary in the extreme. It had not appeared so at the time, and he knew that it was only the contrast with his present existence that made it seem so now. He was living in a kind of fever; he had been in love before—at least, he had imagined himself to be in love—but it had never been like this; this was a feeling of such overwhelming intensity that all else seemed unimportant in comparison.

The effect upon him was so apparent that even Peters noticed it.

'What's happened to you, Mark? You seem to be going round in a daze. You're not putting your mind to your work.'

Peters was right about that. How could his mind be on his work when Juanita had taken permanent possession of it?

But all he said was: 'Are you suggesting I'm not doing my job satisfactorily?'

'Well, you have made a few mistakes lately—rather stupid mistakes—the kind a man makes when he's not really thinking about what he's doing. What's the trouble?'

'No trouble.'

The eyes behind the gold-rimmed glasses peered at him keenly. 'You mustn't let personal problems interfere with your efficiency. Remember it's the Company that pays your salary, and during business hours the Company expects you to give its interests your undivided attention. You do understand that, don't you?'

'I understand it,' Aston said. But whatever the Company might expect, it was not going to make much difference; and quite frankly he did not give two hoots for the Company's expectations, whether it paid his salary or not.

'Incidentally,' Peters said, 'how are relations between you and Miss Merengo coming along?'

Incidentally indeed! As if there could be anything incidental about relations between him and Juanita! As if they could be anything but the whole purpose and meaning of life! But how could Peters, so cold and passionless, be expected to understand that?

He answered evenly: 'They are coming along satisfactorily.' He wondered whether Peters had heard that Juanita was living with him, but it seemed unlikely. Who would have told him? And if he had known he would almost certainly have mentioned the fact, if only to express his disapproval.

'Well,' Peters said, 'whatever you do, be careful. That's my advice—be careful.'

Aston thanked him for the advice.

*   *   *

The question of marriage had come up; indeed, he had himself suggested that they should be married. His great fear was that the affair might not last, that he would lose her. Marriage would have brought stability to the relationship, the kind of permanence he so greatly desired. But Juanita was against it.

'We have each other. We are happy. Isn't that enough?'

'Don't you want to be my wife?'

'I think it is irrelevant.'

'Is it because you are Catholic and I am Protestant? Is that why you won't marry me?'

She laughed at that. 'Do you think I am so primitive? Such things mean nothing to me.'

'Then why?'

'It is better as it is,' she said. 'At least, for the present. If we were to rush into anything now you might regret later that you had been so impetuous.'

'I should never regret marrying you.'

'Ah, you think so now; but time has a way of making words sound foolish.'

'So you don't really love me?'

She took his head between her hands and kissed him.

46

'My darling, what further proof of that do you need? Haven't I given myself to you? What more must I do?'

He answered nothing.

'Aren't you happy with me, Mark?'

'You know I'm happy with you,' he said. And yet he was not sure it was entirely the truth. There was that nagging grain of doubt which made his happiness less than perfect because he felt that it was insecure. And sometimes his love for her was almost like a pain; the very intensity of it made him half afraid; half fearful of a passion that had taken such complete control.

'So no more talk of marriage,' she said; and then, after a while: 'There are other matters that have to be concluded before we think of that.'

'What other matters?'

'You shall see. But no more of that now. Let's talk of other things.'

They talked of other things, but Aston could not rid himself of a feeling of disquiet. Her vague hints, the fact that she had never taken him fully into her confidence even though they were lovers, the secrecy that she still preserved concerning the nature of her work, all this gave him cause for uneasiness. Always there was the faint suspicion that she was withholding from him something that might injure their relationship; and so there remained this vague shadow in the background

47

which he could neither identify nor entirely banish.

Matters remained thus for two or three more weeks, and then one evening Juanita announced suddenly: 'I have invited some people to call. They will arrive at eight o'clock.'

Aston stared at her. It was so unexpected. She had given him no hint that she might be contemplating anything of the kind, and he was not sure that he found it particularly welcome; he would rather have had her to himself. He had been making plans for that evening; now they would all have to be altered.

'What people? Why have you invited them?'

'They wish to talk to you.'

'I don't want to talk to anyone except you,' he said. And then it occurred to him that perhaps here was the dim shadow that was about to step out of the background into full view. He had a presentiment that something was about to happen which might have a profound effect on his life; more specifically on that part of his life which was bound up with Juanita Merengo. And yet there was no solid reason for supposing anything of the kind; she had merely stated that some people were coming to talk to him. Was there anything sinister in that?

'Mark darling,' she said, 'you're not going to be difficult, are you?'

'Difficult?'

'You're not going to slam the door in their faces?'

'Why do they want to talk to me? Do I know them?'

'No, you don't know them; not really.'

'They are friends of yours?'

'Yes.'

He did not like it; he did not want them there. If it had been possible he would have prevented them from coming; but how could he do so now? And was he not being unreasonable? That she should have had friends in Mendoza before joining up with him was only natural; indeed, had she not been with friends at the football match on the day when they had encountered each other in the crowd leaving the stadium? The strange thing was that since then she had never so much as mentioned these friends; it was as though in coming to him she had cast off all other ties.

But apparently it was not so: though she had not mentioned them, she had kept in touch; and now, without even consulting him, she had thrown out this invitation as though the apartment had been her own.

'You should have told me,' he said.

'But I have told you.'

'Earlier. You might have consulted me; at least have warned me.'

'How could I? There has been no opportunity until now.'

'You mean you just happened to meet them

today and so you asked them to come here?'

'Yes.'

It could have been the truth, but there was something odd about it. Yet, though he still did not like it, there was no point in making a fuss and he might as well resign himself. Moreover, some good might come of it; it might lift, if only partially, the veil of obscurity in which Juanita had persisted in shrouding so much of her background. And if he did not like what he saw when the veil did lift, well, that was as it must be.

'There seems to be no way I can avoid seeing them,' he said. 'You've presented me with a *fait accompli*.'

'You make it sound so sinister.'

'And it isn't?'

She put her arms round his neck and kissed him. 'Always remember, my darling, that I love you.'

It seemed to have no relevance to what they had been discussing, but it pleased him to hear her say it. And it might even be the truth. He hoped it was, but he could not be sure. How could anyone ever be certain of a thing like that?

*   *   *

They were punctual guests; they arrived on the stroke of eight. Juanita opened the door to them and they came in one after another—the

50

three of them. Aston looked at them and knew that trouble had walked in. They were the three young men he had seen in The Weeping Crocodile—the fat one, the red-haired one, the coloured one. There was nothing he wished to talk to them about, nothing in the whole wide world.

Juanita introduced them: Enrique Albores, Red McCall, Eduardo Vara. They did not offer to shake hands; they looked at him warily. Vara's eyes had a cold, hard look about them. At a rough guess Aston would have said that Vara hated his guts. For his part he did not feel exactly drawn to Vara either.

'Juanita has told you why we are here?' Albores said.

'She said you wanted to talk to me.'

'That is so.'

'I can't think why.'

'When we have talked you will understand our reasons.'

McCall walked to the window and drew the curtain aside, gazing down at the lamp-lit Avenida Almirante Diaz. He made a soft hissing noise, forcing his breath out between his teeth; then he let the curtain fall back into place, turned and faced the room.

'Yes?' Albores said.

'It'll do, I guess.'

'It will have to do.'

'What are you talking about?' Aston demanded. 'What is this?'

51

'Don't get excited,' Albores said. 'We are going to require this room for one day, that is all.'

'You're going to require what?'

'I think you heard the first time, Señor Aston.'

'I heard,' Aston said. 'But I'm going to need to hear a lot more.' They were certainly cool, walking in like that and informing him that they were going to require the use of his room; not even asking, just stating the bald fact. Who did they think they were? But of course he knew who they were—Juanita's friends; so maybe they thought that gave them some kind of pull. And maybe they were not far off the mark at that.

'Why don't we all sit down?' Albores said. 'You don't mind if we sit down, Señor Aston?'

'Oh, I don't mind. You make yourselves at home. And maybe you'd like some beer.'

It was meant for irony, but it misfired.

Albores smiled, and Aston had to admit that it was a very charming smile, warm and frank and friendly. 'Beer would be most acceptable. Talking can be thirsty work.'

He sat down and the others followed suit. Aston went to the kitchen to fetch the beer, taking Juanita with him. He shut the door and said: 'You didn't tell me it was going to be those three.'

'What do you mean by those three?'

'They're the boys we saw that evening in

52

The Weeping Crocodile. You told me they were not your friends.'

She was getting the cans of beer out of the refrigerator. 'Did I say that?'

'You know damn well you did. You said they were just some people you knew. Now don't tell me you've forgotten.'

'No, I haven't forgotten.'

'So why did you say it?'

'Perhaps because I wanted to keep you all to myself; because I didn't want to go round introducing you to people.'

It sounded flattering, but it also sounded a trifle thin. A thought occurred to him.

'Are these the friends you were with at the football match? The ones you lost touch with.'

'Yes,' she said, 'they are. Does that worry you too?'

'Do you think it should?'

'I don't see why.'

There was no reason; and yet things were stirring in his mind—questions, doubts, uncertainties, suspicions. He wished he had never seen the men; he wished they would melt away and that he would never see them again. But he knew also that it would not work out like that.

They took the beer into the other room. He noticed the way Vara's eyes followed the girl; and he did not like that either.

Albores drank some beer. 'This is good. It is good to be with friends—hospitable friends.'

'You think I am your friend?' Aston said.

'I think you will be, Mark. I may call you Mark?'

'Why not?' Aston drank some beer also, watching Albores. 'Will you tell me why you want the room?' They all gazed at him, saying nothing. When finally Albores spoke it was to ask a question of his own.

'Have you heard of the Feast of the Scorpion?'

Aston nodded. 'I've heard of it. It's a national holiday.' They did themselves pretty well with national holidays in the Republic; there seemed to be a lot of events to commemorate.

'And do you know who the Scorpion was?'

'Some kind of hero—like Admiral Diaz, I believe.'

'His name,' Albores said, 'was Pedro Lopez, but he was known as the Scorpion. Some people would have called him a brigand. Some people did. Today perhaps he would have been called a guerrilla, a freedom fighter. He fought to gain this country's freedom from the Spanish. And he won. On the Tenth of June in the year 1821 he became the first President of the Republic. There was great rejoicing, dancing in the streets, festivity.'

'Which, of course, is why the Tenth of June is known as the Feast of the Scorpion.'

'Exactly. It might have been called Independence Day. Another, larger country to

54

the north celebrates Independence Day, but we prefer our Feast of the Scorpion.'

'This is all very interesting,' Aston said, 'but I still fail to see what it has to do with your wishing to use this room.'

Albores smiled. 'Be patient; I am coming to that. The Feast of the Scorpion is celebrated, as you have said, with a national holiday. There is much festivity; there is a state banquet; there is also a procession, rather like your Lord Mayor's Show in London. The President, of course, leads the procession. The procession passes down the Avenida Almirante Diaz.'

Aston was beginning to understand. 'You are telling me you want to watch the procession from my window? Is that it?'

'That is it,' Albores said; and he lit a cigarette.

McCall began to laugh.

CHAPTER FIVE

INVOLVEMENT

'I don't see why they had to make such a big thing of it,' Aston said. 'I thought they were wanting the room for something important, and it turns out to be just so they can watch a procession from the window. It's crazy.'

55

'But you do not mind?'

The three young men had gone and they were alone in the apartment. The men had not lingered; they had drunk their beer and left. Albores had thanked Aston; McCall had given a nod; Vara had neither spoken nor nodded. Aston had not been sorry to see them go.

'I'm not going to pretend that I'll be overjoyed to have them here; but I could hardly refuse, could I? After all, they are your friends.'

'Yes, they are my friends.'

'I'm a bit puzzled though.'

'What puzzles you, Mark?'

'Well, they didn't strike me as the kind of people who would want to watch processions. I'd have said that sort of thing was hardly in their line.'

'And what,' she asked, 'would you have said was in their line?'

He shrugged. 'Oh, I don't know. Something more active perhaps. If anything was going forward I'd expect them to be taking part in it rather than just looking on. What do they do?'

'Do?'

'For a living. Don't tell me they're gentlemen of leisure.'

She laughed. 'No, they are certainly not that. Far from it.'

'So what do they do?'

He thought she hesitated a moment before answering. Then she said: 'They are partners in a business.'

'What kind of business?'

'Perhaps business is not quite the right word. Perhaps I should have said an enterprise.'

'That's pretty vague.'

'If you with to know more I think you had better ask them.'

'And maybe I wouldn't get any clearer answer if I did.'

'That is possible,' she admitted.

It bothered him. He remembered that impression he had had of trouble walking in when they arrived. The feeling was still with him; he could not shake it off, even though all Albores had asked was that they should be allowed to watch a procession from his window.

'This enterprise,' he said. 'I suppose you wouldn't be a partner in it too?'

'What makes you think I am?'

'I didn't say I thought you were.'

'But you're asking me if I am?'

'Yes.'

She began collecting the empty beer glasses. He watched her in silence, fascinated by every movement she made. She took the glasses to the kitchen and he followed her. She turned the tap on over the sink and started rinsing the glasses. Aston sat on the table, swinging one leg, still watching her.

'You haven't answered the question. Are

57

you a partner in this enterprise?'

She stood the glasses to drain. 'I suppose you could call it that.'

He knew she was not going to tell him what the enterprise was, but he asked her just the same. She turned and put her hands on his arms. She had not dried them and he could feel the moisture through the sleeves of his shirt. She raised herself on tiptoe and kissed him.

'Be patient,' she said; and he remembered that Albores had said that too. 'Be patient, Mark darling. Soon, I promise you, you will know all about it. Very soon. And perhaps when you do know all about it you will not like it so very much.'

He did not like it very much even then. What she had said did nothing to ease his mind. He wondered whether the use of his room had anything to do with the enterprise, but failed to see how that could be possible.

He said: 'I'm not sure I care a lot for Eduardo. The other two seem okay, but Eduardo, he sends cold shivers up my spine.'

'Now you are being fanciful. What have you got against him?'

'Nothing. Except I think he would like to stick a knife in my back and spit on my grave.'

'Oh, Mark!' she said. She was trying to laugh it away, but he fancied she was a shade worried nonetheless. 'What ideas you have! Why would he want to do that?'

58

'Maybe because he's in love with you too.'

She looked startled. 'In love with me!'

'Didn't you know?'

'No,' she said, 'I didn't. And I don't believe it anyway.'

'Are you telling me you haven't noticed the way he looks at you?'

'He looks at everyone the same way.'

'Oh, no, my sweet; that just isn't true. And I think you know it isn't.'

He saw that she was frowning slightly and he guessed that maybe she was casting her mind back and remembering things that had perhaps not seemed significant at the time. Maybe she was seeing Eduardo Vara in quite a new light and was not altogether happy about it. It was strange if she really had not noticed that look in his eyes or had not appreciated its meaning. But people could be blind in some ways.

'He's never said anything then? Never made a pass at you?'

'No,' she said sharply. 'No, of course not.'

'Well, I could be wrong.'

'You are. Yes, I'm sure you are.'

But he knew it was not true. Sure was one thing she was not. Not any more.

*   *   *

It was four days later when they encountered the three men again, and it was in The

59

Weeping Crocodile. It had been Juanita's suggestion that they should go there, and Aston had yielded to her persuasion even though the place did not appeal to him greatly. The fact of the matter was that he guessed Albores and the other two might be there and he had no desire to see them. The Feast of the Scorpion would be quite soon enough for that.

They were sitting at the table in the corner where he had seen them the first time. Albores saw him come in with the girl and he beckoned to them. Aston would have ignored the invitation, but Juanita again persuaded him.

'We must go and speak to them. It would not be polite to refuse to do so.'

He would not have given a damn about politeness, but it was no time to get into an argument. He walked with her to the table in the corner and none of the three seemed at all surprised to see them. There were two spare seats at the table and Aston got the feeling that it had all been arranged beforehand and that Juanita had been in on the arranging.

'This is pleasant,' Albores said. 'This is very pleasant indeed. A meeting of good friends, eh?'

McCall grinned. Vara's face was blankly expressionless.

'You will have some wine?' Albores said.

Before Aston could make a reply Juanita had accepted. 'Thank you, Enrique.'

There was a bottle of wine on the table and

60

two spare glasses. Most certainly it had been prearranged. Albores poured wine for them. He raised his own glass.

'To success!'

'Success in what?' Aston asked.

'In all things,' Albores said.

The steel band was throbbing at the other end of the room; young men and girls were swaying to the rhythm; the air felt like warm treacle.

'You don't look happy, Mark,' McCall said. 'What's eating you?'

'Nothing's eating me,' Aston said.

'Don't you like us?'

'Do you want to be liked?'

'Everyone wants to be liked. It's human nature. Some people even want to be loved; that's a bigger order.'

'All right, Red,' Albores said. 'That's enough of the philosophy.' He turned to Aston. 'It seems to me the time has come for us to be a little more frank with you.'

'I wouldn't disagree with that.'

'You have no doubt been wondering who we really are, what we do for a living, what our background is.'

Aston glanced at Juanita. So she had been talking to them. He wondered just how much of their private conversation she had relayed to these friends of hers. It galled him to think that she should have told them anything.

Albores drank some wine. 'We are idealists.'

Aston raised his eyebrows. 'That's an occupation?'

'Full time but not lucrative.'

Albores seemed to be joking, but Aston sensed an undercurrent of seriousness. It was not entirely a joke. There might be something deadly serious concealed beneath that light-hearted manner.

'What are your aims?'

'Our aims,' Albores said, 'are the same as those which impelled Pedro Lopez to fight the Spaniards one hundred and fifty years ago— freedom and equality.'

'But the country is already free. It is a self-governing republic.'

'Self-governing! Ha!' Vara said. They were the first words he had spoken and they came out like a small explosion.

'The Republic,' Albores said, 'is in the hands of American businessmen. The President is a puppet and it is the C.I.A. that pulls the strings.'

It was no revelation to Aston, the facts were common knowledge. There was scarcely a business of any size that was not an offshoot of an American company; and of those, like Anglo Insurance, that were not, most were British or Japanese. It was a situation that had existed for years: a privileged minority grew rich from it and desired no change; the vast majority endured a low standard of living, complaining but powerless; while a few—

students, Communists, urban guerrillas—resorted to violence in order to bring about a change in the way things were run. But the Government maintained a firm and even savage grip with the help of an armed police force which, in relation to the size of the population, must have been one of the largest in the world. The prisons were full of political prisoners and torture was so commonplace as to be scarcely remarked.

Albores smiled, a little sadly perhaps. 'I think you were already aware of that.'

'And you hope to alter the situation?'

'We can but try. The alternative is despair.'

'You are revolutionaries then?'

'You may call us that if you wish. I prefer the term I used before—idealists.'

Aston felt a chill in his spine like a trickle of ice-cold water; and yet it was so hot in the room that there was sweat on his forehead. Albores spoke with such complete lack of emotion; he might have been revealing nothing more extraordinary than that he and the others belonged to a certain club. Aston had heard of such people; their exploits made headlines in the papers; but he had never before come into personal contact with any of them, and had never really expected to. Certainly he would never have imagined it would be like this, seated round a table in a hot and noisy cellar, drinking wine and listening to the beat of a steel band. Yet it was not this that sent that chilling sensation down his spine; it was the realisation that Juanita was involved, that she was one of them. He glanced at her, then back at Albores.

Albores smiled. 'You begin to understand, I think.'

'Not everything,'

'In time you will.'

Aston was afraid that what Albores said was true; he would perhaps understand only too well. And he was not sure now that he wished to understand.

'You are one of us,' McCall said. 'Now.'

'I am not one of you.'

'In your heart you are,' Albores said; and his voice had a strange persuasiveness. 'In your innermost heart you know that you are in sympathy with us. How could it be otherwise?'

Aston gleaned at Vara and met the man's hard steely gaze. He did not think there was much sympathy between him and Vara.

'You know the cause we fight for is just,' Albores said.

It was the first mention of any fighting and Aston's misgivings increased. Though the word could have been used in its metaphorical sense.

'I don't know anything of the kind. I don't know anything about it. I don't belong in this country; I just work here. It has nothing to do with me.'

'Oh, but it does have something to do with

you. Quite a lot perhaps.' Albores did not turn his head but his eyes moved in Juanita's direction. Aston got the message. Because of her it had to mean something to him. Because she was involved he had to be involved also. Unless he wished to lose her. And that was unthinkable.

'Perhaps,' Vara said, and there was a sneer in his words, 'Señor Aston is afraid to become involved. Perhaps he is a man who likes only the sweet things in life but has not the courage to fight for them. Perhaps he wishes now to withdraw.'

'To withdraw from what?' Aston demanded, staring hard at Vara.

Vara shrugged. 'From involvement.'

Aston had a feeling that Vara would not really be sorry if he pulled out. But how could one pull out of something without fully knowing what that something was? And how, above all, could he show any weakness in front of Juanita with Vara's taunting eyes watching him?

'Are you suggesting I should get up and go?'

'It is for you to choose,' Vara said.

Aston did not move. For perhaps half a minute no one spoke. Then Albores said:

'We are to take it then that you are still willing to allow us to use your room on the Tenth of June?'

'To watch the procession?'

'To watch the procession.'

65

Aston glanced at Juanita. She was gazing steadily at him, waiting for his answer. And if he gave the wrong answer, if he said he was no longer willing to let them have the room, what then? Would she just walk out of the apartment, out of his life, for ever? He was not, could not be, sure. And he dared not take the risk.

'I am willing.'

He heard the girl give a little sigh, as though she had been holding her breath as she waited for his reply. He felt that he had committed himself to something of great importance; and he still did not know precisely what that something was.

He saw the wine-glass in Albores's lifted hand.

'We will drink to it,' Albores said.

*   *   *

She was breathing evenly, but he knew that she was not asleep. Perhaps she found sleep as elusive as he did; perhaps thoughts kept revolving in her mind also, driving sleep away.

'You are awake, Juanita?'

She turned towards him in the darkness, the sheet rustling softly. 'Yes, I am awake. I have been thinking.'

'I have been thinking too.'

'Of what?'

'Of our first meeting.'

66

'Yes?'

'It was no chance encounter, was it? It was planned.'

She did not deny it.

'How did you know I would be at the match?'

'We were told.'

'By whom?'

'Does it matter?'

'No, it doesn't matter.'

No doubt they had been spying on him for weeks, months perhaps. They had studied him, knew his habits, his recreations. He felt a surge of resentment, as though at an invasion of privacy.

'It was all planned, wasn't it? Not just the meeting but what came after. You were to make me fall in love with you. Well, God knows that was easy enough. And you played your part so well; you should have been an actress. Do you know you really had me thinking you felt for me the same way I feel for you? There's a joke.'

He felt the touch of her hand on his arm. 'I love you, Mark, I do love you. You have to believe that.'

'Are you telling me it wasn't planned? That all you said, all you did, was spontaneous.'

She answered almost in a whisper. 'Yes, it was planned. It was planned because of the room, because we had to have the room. But it was not in the plan that I should fall in love with you. That was something which just happened. I couldn't help myself.'

'You expect me to believe that?'

'It is the truth,' she said. 'I love you.'

He wanted to believe it; it was this above all else that he wanted to believe; and yet he had to doubt it. He had been used, was still being used; she had not attempted to deny the fact. How then could he accept her word that, contrary to all expectation, she had fallen in love with him even as he had with her? Would she not be bound to protest as much, if only to ensure his continued co-operation?

'Because I love you,' he said, 'I can refuse you nothing. Can you, for your part, say as much?'

'I don't understand.' She sounded puzzled, but also a little wary, as though she suspected a trap.

'Let me put it like this: if I were to refuse to let your friends use my room on the Tenth of June, would you stay with me just the same?'

She was silent for quite a while, apparently thinking out her answer. Then she said slowly, almost, it seemed, reluctantly: 'No, Mark, I could not do that.'

'So you were lying after all. You don't love me.'

'I was not lying. I do love you. I wish perhaps I didn't, for then it might be easier. But there are some things one has to do, some things one has to fight for whatever the effect

68

may be on one's personal life. You must understand that.'

'No,' he said with a touch of anger, 'I don't understand.' He turned away from her in a gesture of repudiation, but after a time he heard the sound of her voice.

'Mark! Mark darling!'

He did not move. She was putting on the act again, afraid that he might yet pull out, might refuse to let the men use his room. And she was right to be afraid, for that was just what he intended doing. He had been a fool to allow himself to be drawn in this far, but it was not too late to get out. He was not sure quite what it was he had got involved in, but he was damned certain it was not just a matter of three men and a girl watching a procession from a second-floor window. And it was time to put a stop to it—now—before it went any further.

He heard her voice again. 'Mark! Why don't you say something?'

He turned towards her. 'All right, I'll say something. Tomorrow it's finished. Tomorrow you can pack up and go. I never want to see you again.'

'You don't mean that.'

'I do mean it. What makes you so sure I don't?'

'You love me, Mark. You love me too much to send me away.'

She was right. He knew it and it made him

angry. Because of her he had lost the ability to act in a sane and logical way.

'Damn you!' he muttered. 'Damn you!'

He reached out and pulled her to him, crushing her fiercely to him as though with a desire to hurt her, to punish her for what she had done to him. But the other desire was there also, stronger, irresistible as a tide.

'Damn you!' he muttered again, but with a kind of anguish, a kind of despair. 'Damn you!'

He felt the soft pressure of her lips and he knew that some day she might leave him but it would never be he who sent her away, never.

'Damn you, Juanita! Damn you!'

CHAPTER SIX

GUN

It was evening when they came again. Juanita had not told him they were coming, though he guessed she must have known, for when he had suggested going out she had said that she preferred to stay in the apartment. It did not bother him—not until the others arrived.

The door was not locked and they walked straight in, not even troubling to knock.

'Well, make yourselves at home,' Aston said.

It was precisely what they were doing, and he could have saved the sarcasm for a more

70

suitable occasion; it was lost on this one.

Vara closed the door and turned the key in the lock.

'Why that?' Aston asked. He addressed the question to Vara but it was Albores who answered.

'We do not wish to be disturbed.'

'Well, that's nice. Who would be likely to disturb you?'

Albores smiled. 'Who knows?'

McCall was carrying a canvas holdall with a zip fastener. He dumped it on the settee which was pushed up against one wall.

'If you've come to stay,' Aston said, 'I'd better warn you that there aren't any spare beds.'

'I guess there wouldn't be,' McCall said; and he gave a grin.

Vara frowned, as though a thought had angered him.

McCall crossed to the window and adjusted the curtains where a gap was showing. Street-lamps were glittering along the Avenida Almirante Diaz and the faint snarl of traffic was audible in the room. McCall returned to the settee, unzipped the holdall and pulled out two bundles swathed in cloth wrappings. He unwound the wrappings to reveal the stock and barrel of a sporting rifle.

'No,' Aston said. But he had known it would be like this. He had known it while still hoping that it might not be. 'No, not that.'

71

'Now don't pretend you had not already guessed,' Albores said. 'You did not really imagine we simply wished to watch a procession. We are not children and you are not a fool.'

McCall was assembling the rifle with practised fingers, and it was obvious from the way he did it that he was used to handling guns. He took a telescopic sight from the holdall and fixed it to the rifle. The barrel was the colour of wet slate; oily.

'I could tell the police,' Aston said. They were putting themselves in his hands. They must be supremely confident that they had a firm hold on him. Or rather that Juanita had.

'It would not be a healthy thing to do,' Vara said. There was menace in the words and in the way he looked at Aston as he spoke them. 'Not at all a healthy thing.'

McCall did not even look up from what he was doing.

'Certainly you could tell the police,' Albores said, 'but I do not think you will do so. If you betray one of us you betray us all.' His glance shifted to Juanita and back to Aston. 'Would you wish to do that?'

Aston felt trapped. They had him and they knew it. He could not rid himself of them now. If he told them to go they would not do so. The only lever he could use against them was the threat of informing the police, and because of the girl he could never translate such a

72

threat into action. Albores knew it; the others knew it; he had no hope of bluffing them because they had foreseen everything.

'You know what happens to those of us who fall into the hands of the police,' Albores said softly. 'You know what methods of interrogation they use—on men and on women.'

Aston knew only too well—if one could believe the stories. And it was impossible not to believe. Brutality, torture: these were certain to be the lot of Albores and Vara and McCall if he betrayed them. And there would be no possibility of excluding Juanita; she was one of them and she would suffer in the same way; perhaps even more acutely because of her sex. He felt sick when he thought of the things they might do to her, to that sweet body which he loved. It must not come to that.

Albores was looking at him speculatively, reading his thoughts perhaps, smiling faintly. Vara was looking at him too, spitefully, it seemed. Even McCall had lifted his eyes from the rifle. Oh, they knew they had him sure enough; knew it and were glad; gloating maybe at seeing their plan succeeding so easily. Only the girl had turned away as if suddenly ashamed.

'You bastards,' Aston said. 'You scheming rotten bastards. You don't mind who you use, do you?'

'For the cause, no,' Albores said. 'The end

73

justifies any means.'

They were speaking English. Sometimes they used Spanish, alternating between the two languages, both of which they all spoke fluently.

Albores lit one of his cigarettes. McCall had a cigar stuck in the corner of his mouth. Aston looked at the rifle and felt his stomach turn over.

'There must have been other suitable rooms. Why did you have to choose this?'

'We considered all the factors,' Albores said, 'and this one seemed to be the best. Apart from the situation, giving a clear line of sight, there were other advantages.'

'Such as?'

'Such as that you, an Englishman employed by a reputable insurance company, would be unlikely to be suspected of having revolutionary sympathies. The police are not asleep; they will have an eye on any possible sniping points along the route of the procession, but with any luck this will not be rated as a likely one. That was one argument in favour. You yourself were another.'

'I?'

Cigarette smoke dribbled from Albores's mouth and there was laughter in his eyes. 'Young, single, unattached, susceptible—we hoped—to feminine charms.'

Aston again glanced at Juanita. The girl's eyes met his for a moment, dark and troubled;

74

then once more she turned her head away.

'I was an easy target, wasn't I?'

'You were human,' McCall said. 'Male and normal. It happens all the time.'

'We had to make sure of you,' Albores said. 'That was essential to the plan. And how else could we make sure?'

'Well, you did that all right.' Once again Aston looked at Juanita, but she would not meet his eyes. 'It was such sweet bait; how could I resist a nibble? And do you know she actually had me believing she was in love with me? Doesn't that make you laugh?'

'Please!' the girl said, 'Please, Mark!'

'Do we have to listen to all this?' Vara said impatiently.

Aston could see that Vara was pretty tightly wound up and certainly not inclined to any laughter. But he was not concerned with Vara's inclinations.

'You don't have to listen to anything, pal. If you don't like what you hear, nobody's holding you. You can open the door and walk out just whenever you please.'

Vara seemed about to make some angry retort, but as usual Albores stepped in to smooth things over.

'Now let's not start any arguments. That's not going to benefit any of us. Remember we have a job to do.'

'Oh, of course,' Aston said. 'How could anyone forget that? We have to shoot the

75

President.'

McCall gave a sudden laugh. 'You got it wrong. Nobody's aiming to shoot the President. No, sir.'

'No?' Aston was surprised; he had taken it for granted that Carlos Figueiras would be the man, the obvious target for assassination, the symbol of all that a revolutionary must naturally hate.

'No.'

'Then if it's not the President, who is it?'

'The Vice-President,' Albores said.

'But there is no Vice-President.'

'Not of this country, I agree. But there is a Vice-President of the United States.'

Aston stared at him in disbelief and saw that he was not fooling. Albores really meant what he had said.

'But—'

'Surely you have not forgotten,' Albores said, 'that the Vice-President will be here for the celebrations as part of his good-will tour of Central and South America.'

Aston remembered now. How could it have slipped his memory? Certainly it had been enough in the news. But with President Figueiras fixed in his mind as the obvious victim, it had never for a moment occurred to him to look for an alternative. Yet, now that he came to think about it, he saw how much more effective a gesture it would be to kill the Vice-President of the big, powerful country that stood behind the oppressive Government of the Republic. Figueiras was nothing; a well-paid figurehead whose death would only pave the way for another well-paid figurehead to succeed him. But the assassination of the United States Vice-President would cause a far greater stir. It might not—and probably would not—achieve any concrete results in the way of political changes, but as a gesture it would be superb. Besides which, it would undoubtedly bring discredit on the Government and the police of the Republic.

'The Vice-President,' Albores said, 'will be in the Presidential car at the head of the procession.'

Aston thought about it and was appalled. Somehow, it seemed so much worse than the killing of a mere Central American President. This brought the mighty United States fully and openly into the affair. And when the deed had been done, what then? Then there would be a manhunt of such massive proportions that they could scarcely hope to escape. Perhaps to the others that did not seem important; perhaps to them capture and even execution were acceptable if the assassination was accomplished; perhaps they could even contemplate with equanimity and a certain fierce joy the possibility of becoming martyrs to a cause. But that certainly did not go for him; Mark Aston was not of the stuff of which martyrs were made; he had not the taste for the role; he wanted his full share of life, his three score years and ten, if not a shade more.

'And afterwards,' he said, staring into Albores's eyes. 'What happens then?'

Albores gave an airy wave of his cigarette. 'Don't let that trouble you. It is all arranged. We have no intention of allowing ourselves to be captured.'

'You have no intention! Well, that's fine. But suppose it doesn't work out like that.'

'It will work out.' Albores sounded confident. He did not look worried. Aston did not share his confidence, and he was worried enough for all five of them. He turned to McCall.

'What's your stake in this?' It looked as though McCall was going to do the shooting; he was the one who was handling the rifle. He could have been a hired killer, but Aston doubted that. 'Have you got a grudge against the Vice-President?'

McCall was sitting on the settee with the rifle across his knees, one hand resting on the stock and the other on the barrel. His eyes, by some subtle alchemy, seemed to have changed into pale blue lumps of ice; his whole face had hardened, as though turned to rock.

'You ever hear of Vietnam?'

'I heard of it,' Aston said. 'So what?'

'So they sent me there, didn't they?'

'The Vice-President? He sent you?'

'You think it matters two cents who did it?

78

They're all the same, lousy politicians. When I get to thinking of some of the things they made us do out there I feel sick to my stomach. You'd feel sick too. Burning villages, shooting innocent people—old men, women, kids, babies—like they were animals rounded up for slaughter. Rape, murder, torture; you name it, we did it. Man, we were one helluva fine army of bully-boys, executioners, sadists and junkies. Uncle Sam's personal representatives of the democratic civilised way of living. Think like us or we rip your bellies open, burn you with napalm, blow you to bits with high-explosive, take the leaves off your goddamn trees.'

Aston could see that McCall had done things in Vietnam that haunted him. A lot of men probably felt the same way; but with McCall perhaps it went deeper, remained as a canker gnawing away inside him. And someone had to pay for his disgust with himself.

'So you blame the politicians?'

'They sent us there, didn't they? We sure as hell didn't ask to go there.'

'And for that you'll shoot the Vice-President?'

'You're goddamn right I will.'

Aston found it hard to believe that what had begun as such a sweet dream should have turned to this nightmare. Yet it was truly happening; things were moving forward with a kind of inevitability, and because of his love

79

for Juanita he was powerless to stop them.

McCall stood up, the rifle in his hands. 'We gotta find some place to hide this.'

'You're leaving it here?'

'Did you think I brought it just for the fun of carrying it around?'

'But there are still two days to go.'

'Later,' Albores explained, 'it may not be safe. There may be police on the look-out, checking up on what people are carrying. They are bound to take every precaution in view of the importance of the occasion.'

'And suppose they search this apartment?'

'It is quite possible that they will.'

'Which leaves me holding the baby. How do I explain away a high-precision rifle with a telescopic sight?'

Albores smiled. 'It would be difficult, admittedly. Therefore we must make sure it is hidden in a place where they will not find it.'

'You make it sound so easy.'

'Are you afraid?' Vara asked with a sneer.

'You bet your life I'm afraid. And I don't have your fanatical drive. I'm strictly neutral.'

'You are wrong,' Albores said. 'You are not neutral; not any more. You have an interest.'

McCall had put the rifle on the settee and was rolling the carpet back from one side of the room. He tested the floor-boards with his foot and found one that seemed to be loose. He went back to the holdall and took out a hammer and a large screwdriver. With the screwdriver he began levering up the loose floor-board, taking care not to make any marks on the wood. The board came up without much difficulty; it was only a short piece which looked as though it might have been put in to replace part of an older board that had perhaps rotted. A faint odour of dry rot came up from the cavity.

McCall dismantled the rifle and pushed the separate parts into the spaces between the joists, reaching in to the full length of his arm, so that it was impossible to see any sign of them when he had finished. He took a box of ammunition from the holdall and hid that too. Finally he replaced the board and pulled the carpet over it.

Aston felt as though a bomb had been planted in his room. 'Suppose they bring metal detectors.'

'It's not likely,' Albores said, 'You must remember that they have no reason to suspect you.'

'I'm afraid I don't find that particularly reassuring. They're not going to take anyone's innocence on trust.'

'You worry too much,' McCall said. 'Nobody's going to find the gun.' He turned to Albores. 'Let's go. The less time we spend here, the better.'

Albores agreed. 'There's nothing else to do now except wait. We'll be seeing you, Mark— on the Tenth. Take care of yourself.'

'I'll try not to fall under a bus,' Aston said. 'For your sake.'

McCall laughed; Albores smiled; Vara looked unamused. McCall picked up the holdall. Vara unlocked the door and they went away. Aston wished they might never come back, but he knew they would.

*   *   *

The girl avoided looking at him when they had gone. She went into the bedroom and after a while he followed her. She was sitting perfectly motionless in front of the dressing-table and staring at the reflection in the glass. He came up behind her and rested his hands lightly on her shoulders. She shivered slightly but said nothing.

'Well?' he said. 'Are you satisfied?'

Her eyes met his reflected in the glass. 'Satisfied?'

'You've got what you wanted. You've got me entangled in this hare-brained scheme. So now are you satisfied? Are you happy?'

'I am not happy,' she said.

'No? You should be; you should be jumping for joy. Tell me why you're not happy when everything has gone exactly according to plan.'

'It is because of you.'

'Me? What have I done to spoil things? I've played it your way all along the line, haven't I? What more could you ask of me?'

'Forgiveness perhaps.' Her voice so low now, it was scarcely audible.

'Ah, that!' He took his hands from her shoulders, walked to the bed and sat down. One of the springs in the mattress made a twanging sound like a plucked guitar. 'Why that now?'

'I tricked you, Mark.'

'Well, of course you tricked me. It's what you were meant to do.'

'And now I feel ashamed.'

He stared at the back of her head, wondering whether to believe her; and wondering, too, whether she would have gone through the same performance with any other man, if that other man had had the room they needed. It hurt him to think so, but what else could he think?

'Suppose it had been someone else,' he said, probing the wound. 'Not me. Would you still have gone through with it? Everything?'

She saw what he was getting at and seemed embarrassed.

'I don't know.'

'What do you mean, you don't know?' His voice hardened. 'Of course you'd have done it. It was just a job, wasn't it?'

'Don't say that,' she said. 'Don't say that.'

'Why not? It's true, isn't it?'

'It was true at first perhaps. But later—with you—it was so much more; oh, so very much more. A joy and a pain. Don't you

83

understand?'

'Well, maybe so. But all the same, if it hadn't been me, if it had been someone else, you'd still have gone through with it?' He could not stop worrying at the question, though it tormented him. 'Isn't that so?'

Her shoulders seemed to droop a little. The answer came like a sigh: 'Yes, I suppose so.'

'Ah!' He brought his clenched fist down on the bed, drawing another twang of protest from the mattress. He stood up and walked to the door, then turned and faced her. 'You're no better than a whore, are you?'

Her head turned swiftly. Tears had dribbled down her cheeks, but now her eyes flashed with sudden anger. 'You have no right to say that. No, no, no! Not that! Not ever!'

He regretted immediately what he had said. He moved towards her. He reached out as though to put a hand on her arm, but she brushed it aside with a gesture of rejection and her eyes still burned with that sudden fire.

'Is that what you think of me?'

'Does it matter what I think?' he asked wearily.

'It matters to me. Do you really think I am that?'

He shook his head. 'No, Juanita; it was a word spoken in anger.' Again he moved his hand to touch her arm, and this time she did not thrust it away. 'How could I think that when I love you so much?'

The fire died out of her eyes, leaving only the tears. She put her hand on his. 'Perhaps you had some reason. You have been badly treated.'

He made as if to speak, but she went on quickly: 'It is so, and you have good cause to despise me—'

'I don't despise you.'

'I am glad,' she said, 'but nevertheless, you have cause and I cannot deny it. You have asked me whether I would have done the same if it had been another man. I might have—for the sake of what I believe in—but truly I cannot say for certain. Is it possible to predict just how one will act in a particular situation? But of this I am sure: whatever the end in view, whatever the pressure that might be brought to bear, if a similar situation were to arise again, I could not do it.'

'No?'

'No.'

'Why not, Juanita?'

'Do you need to ask? Haven't I told you I love you? Do you imagine I could give myself to any other man now?'

Again he wondered whether she was telling the truth, but he looked into her eyes and could not help believing. And perhaps he believed her more easily because he wished to do so.

He kissed her and she clung to him passionately, as though fearful that he might slip away; but nothing was further from his mind. He wanted her and could not imagine a time when he would cease to want her. But then he remembered the rifle under the floor-boards and his heart gave a lurch. Why in hell did it have to be like this?

'It will be all right,' the whispered. 'I promise you everything will be all right. You don't need to worry.'

The Vice-President of the United States was going to be shot down from the window of his apartment and she said he had no need to worry. That was a laugh—if he had felt like laughing.

'You're mad,' he said. 'We're all mad, Juanita; you and I and Enrique and Red and Eduardo. We're driving headlong to disaster like a car with the steering gone, and no one has got the sense or the guts to put his foot on the brake.'

He felt a tremor run through her body, but she said nothing. Perhaps this time she felt unable to dispute the truth of what he had said. Perhaps she too had glimpsed the dark pit that was waiting to swallow them.

CHAPTER SEVEN

SEARCH

She was making coffee in the kitchen. Aston could smell the coffee and also the scent of the toilet soap she had used for her bath; the two odours mingled sweetly and he felt the delight of having her there, and then the quick surge of apprehension as he recalled what was so soon to happen.

It was the morning of the Ninth of June. One more day. There was a sick flutter in his stomach.

'We could still pull out,' he said. 'You know that, don't you?'

'We can't pull out now,' she said. 'It is all arranged.'

'To hell with its being arranged. We could ditch the rifle and the ammo. They could do nothing then. It would be the sensible thing to do.'

She turned her head and stared at him, eyes wide. 'You're not serious about this, are you, Mark?'

'You bet I'm serious. I've never been more serious in my life.'

'We couldn't do that.'

'Why not? Give me one good reason why we couldn't do it.'

'It would not be loyal.'

'Damn loyalty. I don't owe anyone any loyalty.'

'But I do, Mark.'

'Why don't you forget all that nonsense? Who owes loyalty to a bunch of assassins?'

'I am one of that bunch of assassins,' she said. 'Have you forgotten?'

'Then get out of it—now—while you've still got the chance. Get out of it, for God's sake.'

'Are you asking me to desert my friends?'

'I'm asking you to have a bit of sense before it's too late. You'd be helping them really.'

She sighed. 'We've been over this so many times, and it's no use. I can't draw back now; I have to go on to the end.'

Aston sighed also. 'And I have to go on to the end with you.'

*   *   *

He ran across Peters during the lunch break.

Peters said: 'You look a bit under the weather, Mark. Too many late nights?'

'Could be,' Aston said.

'You should watch it. Don't want you turning up sick.'

Aston gave a phoney laugh. 'Not much fear of that.'

'I hope not.' Peters gave him a searching look, then said: 'Eva's been inquiring about you.'

'About me?'

'She wants to know when you're going to get married.'

Aston stared. 'Married!'

'To Miss Merengo.'

'Oh.'

'Eva's a great little match-maker, and you know she's taken a liking to Juanita.'

'Well, I'll let you know if anything moves.'

'Yes, do,' Peters said. 'And by the way'—He lowered his voice to a more conspiratorial level—'have you discovered anything more concerning her—um—background?'

'No,' Aston said, 'I haven't.'

'Well, be careful.' Peters looked a shade worried. 'I'd hate to see you get into any kind of trouble.'

Aston gave another of the phoney laughs, which might or might not have fooled Peters. 'No need to bother yourself on that score. I'm not going to get into any trouble.'

He was not at all sure that Peters was fooled; the deputy manager's expression seemed to register a certain amount of doubt, even some misgivings, and Aston wondered, a trifle uneasily, whether Peters had been doing a bit of private investigation regarding Juanita and the kind of people she associated with. And whether he had come up with any disturbing facts. But it seemed inadvisable to ask him.

'Well,' Peters said, 'you've got a day off

tomorrow, and my advice is to take it easy. You don't have to go celebrating wildly even if it is the Feast of the Scorpion. All that nonsense doesn't mean a thing to us, does it?'

'No,' Aston said, 'it doesn't mean a thing to us.'

And by God, how he wished that were true!

*   *   *

When the office closed Aston went straight back to the apartment. The tram was crowded as usual at that hour when all the business houses were disgorging their workers, and he had to stand, crushed between a large fat woman with a greasy copper skin and a sad-looking man with a beaked nose and a mat of coarse black hair. The woman's ample bosom was pressing against his lower ribs, and every time the tram gave a lurch the pressure was increased. He found the situation both uncomfortable and embarrassing, and it was with some relief that he left the tram, feeling limp and a trifle damp, like a dish-cloth that had just done a spell of work.

There seemed to be even more police than usual on the streets; though it might have been simply that in his present uneasy frame of mind he took more notice of them. The Mendoza police had never produced in Aston the feeling of security that police in England did. They were as heavily armed as brigands, were seldom as well shaved as might have been expected, and had a way of lounging against walls in little menacing groups with cigarettes dangling from their lips. Aston had never come across an ordinary citizen who did not regard them as more of a threat than a safeguard, and he could understand the reason why.

He was stopped and searched for weapons on the Avenida Almirante Diaz and was forced to produce his passport before being allowed to proceed on his way. He was sweating when he reached the apartment.

Juanita was already there, waiting for him.

'I was stopped by the police,' he said. 'In the street. They frisked me. I had to show my passport.'

She was less impressed than he had expected. 'They're checking up. Lots of people have been stopped. I was.'

'You!'

She smiled. 'Why not? Why should I be exempt?'

'And they passed you?'

'Again why not? I am not a criminal.'

Her coolness amazed him. How could she accept so calmly something that had made his scalp crawl and caused him to sweat at every pore?

'And you are not on any list of suspects?'

'I have no reason to believe that I am. I have never been in any kind of trouble with the police.'

'Have the others?'

'None of them has ever been arrested.'

'That could soon be altered,' Aston said. 'For all of us.'

'Don't be so pessimistic, Mark. Everything is going to be all right.'

'I'll bet Jael said that to Sisera before she hammered the nail into his head.'

'Nobody's going to hammer a nail into your head, Mark darling.'

'A bullet can be just as effective,' Aston said, and left her to think that over while he took a shower.

*   *   *

He was drinking a glass of cold beer and beginning to feel slightly less jumpy when the sound of heavy feet on the landing outside the room and the insistent ringing of the door-bell put him back where he had started.

Juanita opened the door and two policemen walked in without even waiting for an invitation. One was tall and lean, with a narrow, seamed face like a piece of rock that had taken a lot of weather; his hair was beginning to grey at the temples and his shoulders lifted his shirt like hidden props. The other man was younger, thicker, not so tall; he had a handsome face and he grinned a lot, as if he enjoyed his work.

92

'We have to search the apartment,' the older man said. He referred to a slip of paper in his hand, a list of some kind. 'You are Señor Aston—the tenant?'

'Yes.'

'And this is perhaps Señora Aston?'

'No. This is Señorita Merengo.'

'A friend?'

'Yes.'

'Ah, so.'

The younger man was still grinning, rather more perhaps. His eyes seemed to be stripping the girl and his lips were moist. Aston began to hate him.

'You have no objection,' the older man said, 'to our searching the apartment?'

'Would it make any difference if I had?'

The bony shoulders rose a little higher. 'It is routine. It has to be done because of tomorrow's procession, you understand.'

'I understand,' Aston said. 'You would perhaps like a glass of beer.' He was not sure whether it was wise to make the offer. Would the policeman's suspicions be aroused by so obvious an attempt at ingratiation?

But all the man said was: 'Thank you, señor. It is indeed thirsty work.'

'And you?' Aston turned to the younger man, who, with some reluctance it seemed, dragged his eyes away from the girl.

'I also could drink a glass of beer.' His grin as he said it seemed to mock Aston. He looked

93

to be full of mockery and not to be trusted an inch.

'I will fetch the beer,' Juanita said. She went into the kitchen.

The younger policeman followed her. Aston could hear a murmur of voices, then the sound of a scuffle and of glass breaking. He began moving towards the door of the kitchen, but the bony policeman stopped him.

'I will go.'

He went into the kitchen and a moment later the younger man appeared, and he was no longer grinning. Juanita and the bony policeman followed. The girl was carrying two glasses of beer which she set down on the table with a thump that caused some of the liquid to spill over. There was a high colour in her cheeks and she looked angry. The bony policeman picked up the glasses and handed one to his companion. He spoke roughly.

'Here! Drink!'

The younger man seemed half inclined to refuse the beer, but the bony policeman gave him a stare and he took it sulkily. They both drank rapidly and then began the search. Aston reflected gloomily that things could hardly have had a less auspicious start. He ought not to have offered any beer, but how could he have foreseen that the younger policeman would make a pass at Juanita?

It was a thorough search; the men gave the impression that they had been through the routine many times and knew all the likely hiding-places for illegal weapons. Aston tried to avoid letting his gaze stray to that part of the floor under which the rifle was hidden, but he found it difficult to do so; his eyes seemed to be drawn to the spot as if by a kind of magnetism. Fortunately, no one appeared to notice.

The search of the living-room was soon completed and nothing had been found. The scene of operations shifted to the bedroom. The two policemen worked in moody silence while Aston and the girl looked on. The bedroom was cleared, then the bathroom and the kitchen. They returned to the living-room.

'Are you satisfied?' Aston inquired.

The bony policeman shrugged. 'We have found nothing.'

'There is nothing to find.'

'That is as it should be.'

The younger policeman was moving restlessly about the room; the grin had not returned to his face and he looked sullen— dangerous perhaps. Aston wished both of the men would go; he had been on edge all the while they had been there.

Suddenly the younger policeman came to a halt, and Aston saw that he was standing just where the rifle was hidden. He seemed to be testing the floor with his foot.

'There is a loose board here,' he said.

'There are a lot of loose boards,' Aston said.

'I have felt no others.' He looked at the older policeman. 'I think we should look into this.'

'We have other apartments to search.'

'This will not take long.'

'Well, if you must; but you will find nothing.'

'Of course you will find nothing,' Aston said, 'Do you imagine I hide things under the floor?'

He knew at once that it had been the wrong thing to say. He saw the sudden flicker of suspicion in the bony policeman's eye.

'You do not wish us to take up the floor-board?'

'Does anyone enjoy having his floor ripped up?'

'No; no one does. But some people have more reason to object to it than others. Are you one of those people?'

Aston shrugged, attempting a show of indifference. 'Go ahead if you wish.'

'We will do so,' the bony policeman said.

The younger man rolled the carpet back and inserted the blade of a heavy knife in the gap between the boards. The loose board came up easily, revealing the empty cavities beneath.

'You see,' Aston said. 'There is nothing.'

'I do not see,' the bony policeman said. 'Not yet.'

The younger man was down on his knees, feeling in the spaces between the joists. Aston waited. He felt that it was all up now; the rifle would be found; he and Juanita would be arrested. And the others? He would make damned certain they did not get off; he owed them no loyalty and he would spill it all; there would be no need for any torture to make him talk.

'Ah!' It was the younger policeman uttering a low exclamation of triumph, he had found something. Slowly he withdrew his arm, perhaps savouring the drama of the moment, and he was grinning again. His hand came into view and the object that was in it. Then suddenly, with a gesture of disgust, he threw the thing from him. It landed almost at Aston's feet and he saw that it was the whitened skeleton of a very large rat.

The bony policeman began to laugh. The younger man was cursing.

They went away without even bothering to replace the loose floor-board. Aston could hear the sound of their feet clumping down the stairs.

*   *   *

'We have made an enemy,' he said.

'He is not important.'

'All enemies are important. Especially policemen.'

'It cannot be helped.'

'What happened in the kitchen?'

97

She hesitated a moment. Then: 'He took liberties.'

'You mean he tried to kiss you?'

'It was more than that.'

'And you hit him?'

'Yes.'

'That wasn't a wise thing to do.'

'I was not thinking about the wisdom of it.'

'It could have been fatal. It made him angry. If he had not been so angry I don't think he would have bothered about the floor. He wanted to get his own back.'

'Are you saying I should have let him do as he wished?' She was becoming a little angry herself.

Aston was still feeling pretty shaken by the experience he had been through and he could not resist making a thrust at her. 'I thought perhaps you would have done it for the sake of the cause.'

Her eyes flashed. 'Perhaps you wish I had. Perhaps you think only of saving your own skin.'

'If I thought only of that I wouldn't be in this thing at all.'

Her anger died as quickly as it had risen. 'I am sorry. I should not have said what I did.'

'And I shouldn't have said what I did. There's no sense in our snarling at each other. It's this damned tension—building up.'

'I know, Mark darling, I know. But soon it will be over. Very soon now.'

And what then? he thought. Even if they got away after the killing, they would be fugitives, hunted remorselessly, with no place to hide. It was a pretty bleak future.

But all he said was: 'Yes, soon it will be over.'

*   *   *

He lay awake in the darkness, tormented by thoughts about the morrow. Beside him the girl was sleeping peacefully, and he wished he could have faced things with as much equanimity as she apparently did. A thousand times he pictured the fatal moment when the Vice-President should be struck by the bullet. He imagined the tumult, the swarms of police, the immediate search for the killers. And then the flight, the pursuit, the terror of being a hunted animal; and finally capture, a brief trial for appearances' sake, and execution.

But it did not have to come to that. It was still possible to thwart Albores and the others. He had only to get rid of the rifle: without that there would be no killing; the procession would roll on its way and no harm would be done. Except that he would have lost Juanita.

Yet was even that certain? Not if she loved him as she had said; and as he now believed she did. Surely she would not leave him even if he ditched the rifle. And he would perhaps have saved her life; he had to think of that aspect; it was her life as well as his own that was at risk if this crazy scheme was carried through to its bloody conclusion.

He came to a decision: he would do it; he would do it now while there was still time. He had delayed long enough; it was already three in the morning.

He slipped carefully out of bed, taking pains not to wake the sleeping girl. She made a slight movement and sighed; he froze for an instant, but then her breathing returned to normal and he knew that she was still asleep. A moment later he was out of the bedroom and had silently closed the door.

The living-room light came on as his fingers touched the switch, and he quickly rolled back the carpet. He found a screwdriver in the kitchen and the board came up easily, the nails scarcely holding at all. He laid it on one side, lay down on the floor and groped for the rifle. McCall had pushed the dismantled weapon as far as possible into the cavities, and it was just as well that he had done so, otherwise the young policeman might have found it instead of the rat's skeleton. McCall had long arms, and Aston had to stretch out his fingers to their fullest extent before he could get a grip on the gun. But he finally got it out, all of it, including the telescopic sight and the box of ammunition. The collection of pieces that, once assembled, would become a lethal weapon capable of shaking the Republic to its foundations lay on the bare floor, and only then did it occur to him that he would need something in which to carry them.

He went back into the kitchen and found a large bag made of tough brown paper that had contained potatoes. There were still a few remaining in it and he tipped them into a bowl before returning to the living-room.

Juanita was standing in the doorway to the bedroom, staring at the dismantled rifle.

Aston came to a halt with the paper bag dangling in his left hand, feeling foolish. Juanita looked at him.

'What are you doing?'

'I'm ditching the rifle.'

'No,' she said, 'you cannot do that.'

'I can. I should have done it sooner. We had a narrow shave with those policemen, but not again. This time I'm going to put a stop to the nonsense, once and for all.'

'What do you intend doing with the rifle?'

'I'll find somewhere to dump it.'

'If you're going out,' she said calmly, 'you'll need to dress. Unless you mean to go like that.'

'Of course I don't mean to go like this.'

'And when the police stop you and want to know what you're carrying in the parcel at this time of night, what do you tell them?'

'The police!'

'They'll be patrolling. Anyone moving around at this hour is bound to be picked up

101

and questioned. Especially someone carrying a gun wrapped up in a paper bag. Hadn't you thought of that?'

He had not. Now that she mentioned it, he wondered how he could have failed to do so. It was as certain as anything could be that police activity would continue throughout the night, and the thought of being stopped with the rifle in his possession brought him out in a cold sweat of apprehension. What could he possibly say that would have the smallest trace of plausibility?

Of course he might get through without being challenged—if he were lucky; but could he take that risk? For all he knew, there might be policemen stationed all along the Avenida Almirante Diaz; he might be picked up before he had taken half a dozen paces.

'Don't you think you had better change your mind?' Juanita said gently.

He stood there undecided, with the paper bag still gripped in his left hand, feeling the grain of the floor-boards under his bare feet and staring at the girl across the width of the room. Then, abruptly, he turned and went back into the kitchen. He tipped the potatoes out of the bowl and into the bag and returned to the living-room.

Juanita had not moved. He picked up the rifle barrel and pushed it into the space between the joists from which he had taken it. He did the same with the stock and the telescopic sight and the box of ammunition. He replaced the board and tapped in the nails. He unrolled the carpet and smoothed it out with his foot.

'You see,' he said, with a sardonic twist of the mouth. 'I always take your advice.'

'Come back to bed,' she said. 'You should try to get some sleep.'

He followed her into the bedroom. He was overwhelmed by a feeling of helplessness. Whatever he did now, the assassination would take place. It was as inevitable as the rising of the morning sun.

CHAPTER EIGHT

TENTH OF JUNE

'What time will they come?' he asked.

'I don't know,' she said. 'But they will not be late.'

'For my money they couldn't be too late.'

He had slept only in brief snatches, plagued by nightmares from which he awoke sweating and trembling, his mouth dry and his heart thumping. Sitting at the small table in the kitchen, trying to eat some breakfast, he felt completely wretched. He pushed the half-eaten sausage away and drank some coffee.

'You don't look well,' she said.

103

'I don't feel well. I didn't sleep.'

'I know. You were tossing and turning all night. You kept groaning too.'

'How do you know? You were sleeping.'

'No,' she said, 'I did not sleep either.'

'I thought you were asleep.'

'Well, perhaps a little, but not much.'

'So you were worried too?'

'Who would not be? But it will be all right.'

'Oh, sure it will,' he said. 'The Vice-President will be dead and everything in the garden will be lovely. You're crazy, do you know that? You're all crazy. And I'm crazy too.'

He finished his coffee and went into the living-room and stared out of the open window. Along the Avenida Almirante Diaz the lamp-standards had been decorated with coloured streamers so that they looked like barbers' poles and there were a lot of flags hanging out; everywhere the tricolour of the Republic and the Stars and Stripes of the United States were to be seen, and there were even a few Union Jacks here and there. The sun was already hot and there was scarcely a breath of wind; the flags hanging limply in the still air. On the other side of the street a second-floor balcony was bright with flowers, and Aston saw a girl of ten or eleven come out from the room behind and glance first one way and then the other, as though expecting the procession to come at any moment. He could

104

see her quite clearly; she had dark hair twisted into pigtails and tied with ribbons so that it stuck out on each side of her head, and she was wearing a red and white dress drawn in at the waist with a belt and then flaring out like a ballet dancer's. It looked like a party dress, and had perhaps been bought specially for the occasion.

And what an occasion it was going to be!

The girl suddenly caught sight of him watching her. She waved her hand. Aston waved back; which seemed to delight the child, for she followed this up with a perfect frenzy of waving, jumping up and down on the balcony and finishing with a kind of Highland fling.

Aston wished that he could have faced the day in such high spirits: for the child it was a holiday; for him it was a day of foreboding. He gave a final brief wave of the hand and turned away from the window.

Juanita was busy in the kitchen; he could hear the sounds of plates and cups being washed, and that song again—the one he had taught her, which she liked so much. She was crooning it softly, but he could hear the words.

'Alas! my love, you do me wrong
To cast me off discourteously;
And I have lovéd you so long,
Delighting in your company.
Greensleeves was all my joy!

105

Greensleeves was my delight!
Greensleeves was my heart of gold!
And who but my Lady Greensleeves!'

He would have to leave the guitar of course. There were other things he would have to leave—books, most of his clothing, various possessions that he had gathered around him during his time in Mendoza, souvenirs that he had intended taking back to England; all these would have to be abandoned. A fugitive must travel light.

He became aware that the song had ended. She was standing in the doorway of the kitchen, watching him.

'You're restless,' she said. 'I wish you would relax.'

He stared at her. 'How can you sing at a time like this? Doesn't it bother you at all?'

'It bothers me. I try not to think about it too much. Singing helps.'

He pointed towards the window. 'There's a child out there—on the balcony across the street; she's dressed up for the occasion; she waved to me.'

'So?'

'What's it going to be like for her, seeing a man killed? What's it going to do to her, to her mind? Have you thought of that?'

'Even children must learn that life is not all play.'

'They shouldn't have to learn like this.'

'I think you have to learn too,' she said. 'You have to realise it is not all strumming guitars and singing folk songs. This is a hard world.'

'Don't talk to me as though I were a child,' he answered angrily. 'I know what the world is. I know it could be better. And I know that it is never made better by assassination.'

'Perhaps you are right,' she said with a sigh. 'And that is a sad thing too. But now I think you had better pack.'

It was pointless to argue about it any further; they had been over all the arguments already. He went into the bedroom and began putting the few essential things he would be taking in the cheap duffle-bag which he had bought for the purpose.

*   *   *

They did not arrive together. Albores was the first to come. He looked hot but unworried. He gave Juanita a brotherly kind of kiss and strolled to the window.

'So the day has arrived.'

'It's a habit days have,' Aston said.

Albores left the window, sat down, pulled out a packet of cigarettes and offered them to the others. Both refused. Albores took a cigarette for himself.

'You do not object?'

'It's not smoking I object to,' Aston said.

107

Albores raised his eyebrows a little. 'You are not still bothered by this affair?'

'Does it surprise you?'

'But I have told you there will be no trouble.'

'We've already had trouble.'

Albores's head jerked slightly and he did not look quite so complacent. 'You have?'

Aston told him about the policemen. Albores smoked his cigarette and listened in silence until Aston had finished.

Then he said: 'I did not think they would get so close. It was certain that they would search, but to get as close as that! Everything might have been ruined.'

'Juanita and I could have been arrested.'

'Of course,' Albores said; but it was obvious that he considered that a minor point.

Aston was needled by Albores's attitude and decided to shake him a little more.

'I tried to dump the gun.'

'You did what?' Albores sat up in his chair.

'I tried to dump the gun.'

'When? How?'

'Last night. I'd had enough. It would have been a way of stopping you. I took it out of the floor; I even got as far as finding a bag to put it in.'

'What were you going to do with it?'

'I don't know. Throw it away somewhere.'

'And why didn't you?'

'Juanita woke up and saw what I was doing.

108

She persuaded me to abandon the idea.'

'I told him the police would be bound to stop him,' Juanita said. 'It was no more than the truth.'

'Yes,' Albores said, 'it would have been a foolish thing to try.' He stared hard at Aston. 'You would have betrayed us?'

'Why talk of betrayal?' Aston spoke impatiently. 'You would have been safe enough. Safer. You would simply not have been able to go through with your plan.'

'That would have been betrayal,' Albores said. He took some more smoke from the cigarette, thinking. 'It might be well not to mention this to the others. It would cause hard feeling. Red and Eduardo might not be as understanding as I. Especially Eduardo. He has no liking for you, I think.'

'I have no liking for him.'

'Well, do not go out of your way to cross him. There may come a time when your life rests in his hands.'

*   *   *

McCall was the next to arrive.

'Man,' he said, 'they're sure getting jumpy. I was stopped on the street; had to show my passport and all that jazz. Then they frisked me. Lucky I was clean.'

'I was stopped yesterday,' Aston said. 'They gave me the treatment too.'

'Do you think they suspected you?' the girl asked. She looked at McCall with a faintly worried expression on her face.

'Hell, no,' McCall said. 'It was just routine, I guess. They're checking up left, right and centre. They're dumb bastards though.'

'Don't underrate them,' Albores warned him. 'They're not all so dumb.'

'Sure, sure. I guess not.'

McCall also went to the window and looked out. 'Decorations, for Pete's sake,' he said. 'Day of rejoicing. What have they got to rejoice about? The chance of seeing the Vice-President of the United States! Big deal!'

'They'll have something to rejoice about later,' Albores said.

'If they've got the sense to appreciate it.' He came away from the window. 'It's like we could be doing this for a bunch of morons who don't know left from right.'

'We're doing it for future generations,' Juanita said.

'Is that so? Well, maybe that goes for you, sweetheart, but not for me. I'm doing this for me; nobody else.'

'Working off a grudge?' Aston said.

'That's right—working off a grudge. Any objections?'

'Plenty, but you've already heard them.'

They were all crazy, and maybe when you really got down to it McCall was the craziest of the lot.

'I'm going to take a shower,' the girl said.

She went into the bedroom. A minute later Vara arrived.

'You have any trouble?' McCall asked.

'Trouble!' Vara said. 'Why should I have trouble?'

'They're stopping people in the streets.'

'I wasn't stopped,' Vara said.

'Where did you leave the car?' Albores asked.

'The place we arranged. It's all right.'

'It had better be,' McCall said. 'Just too bad if somebody stole it.'

'Who'd steal a car like that?' Vara's gaze flickered round the room. 'Where's Juanita?'

Albores gave a jerk of the head in the direction of the bedroom. 'She went to take a shower.'

Vara glanced at Aston. 'You don't look so good.'

'I didn't sleep well.'

'Feeling scared?'

'You might say that.'

'It is natural,' Albores said.

'Are you scared?' Aston asked.

Albores smiled. 'Of course. We are all scared. How could it be otherwise?'

'I am not,' Vara said.

'No? Then you are the exception.'

'He's scared too,' McCall said. 'He's just too damned proud to admit it.'

'I am not,' Vara said again; and he looked

111

angry.

'Okay. Don't get hot round the neck. Have it your own way, hero.'

'If you're so scared,' Vara said, 'maybe you don't shoot so good.'

'You don't need to worry about that,' McCall told him. 'Nothing affects my aim.'

'We don't have any proof of that.'

'You'll get your proof of it soon enough.' McCall was becoming heated also. 'I learnt my lessons in a tough school. So don't bother your head about my side of the contract, Eddie boy; you just keep your mind on your driving.'

Aston could see that Vara resented being talked to in that way. He scowled and chewed his lip, but apparently came to the conclusion that it was not worth while continuing the argument.

From the bathroom came the sound of the shower, and then of the girl singing.

'Alas! my love, you do me wrong
To cast me off discourteously . . .'

CHAPTER NINE

VISITORS

The door of the kitchen opened and Vara was standing there. He said with a hint of venom:

112

'I thought it was to make sandwiches that you came in here, but it seems you have more important matters to attend to.'

Aston turned and stared at Vara. 'Are you so hungry you can't wait for a few minutes?'

'There is hunger and hunger,' Vara said, and he looked at the girl with sombre eyes.

She had stopped to pick up the knife she had dropped. The loose bathrobe fell open and her breasts were uncovered for a moment before she straightened again and quickly adjusted the garment.

Vara seemed to be breathing harder. 'Is that the way you flaunt your nakedness like a common whore?'

Her fingers tightened on the knife, as though she would have stabbed him with it. 'You dare to call me that!'

'Isn't it what you have become?'

Aston clenched his fist, ready to strike Vara. Yet he had used almost the same words himself. He did not move.

'No,' the girl said in a voice that trembled with anger, 'it is not what I have become. And who are you to criticise even if it were? At whose suggestion, at whose urging would it have been?'

'Not mine,' Vara said. 'Never at mine.' He gazed at her and seemed to be in pain.

'You'd better go,' Aston said.

'So that you two can carry on amusing yourselves?' Vara's tone was bitterly sarcastic.

'Aren't the nights long enough for you?'

Juanita took a step towards him, bringing them face to face. 'What's troubling you, Eduardo? Why are you so concerned about what I do?'

He did not answer. He was trembling slightly. He could not keep his hands still.

'I make my own decisions,' she said. 'It is not for you to tell me how to conduct myself.'

'It should not be like this,' he muttered. 'Not like this.'

'Go back into the other room, Eduardo. We will bring the food.'

He turned suddenly and left the kitchen.

Juanita looked at Aston with a troubled frown. 'What's wrong with him?'

'I told you,' Anon said. 'He's in love with you and he's as jealous as hell. It's like a rat gnawing at his guts and it puts the knife in him to see you with me. In his place I'd feel the same.'

'Oh, God,' she said, 'as if we needed complications like that!'

'You'd better finish cutting the sandwiches.'

'And you'd better finish pouring the beer. And this time keep your hands off me.'

*　　　*　　　*

When they went into the living-room Vara was standing at the window staring silently down on the Avenida Almirante Diaz. McCall was

114

smoking a cigarette and Albores was slumped in the chair where they had left him, his eyes closed as though he were dozing. He woke up quickly enough when the food and drink appeared.

Juanita put the plate of sandwiches on the table and said she would go and dress.

'You do not wish to eat?' Albores asked.

'I will have a sandwich when I have dressed.' She shot a glance at Vara. 'Eduardo does not approve of me as I am.'

McCall grinned. 'You look fine to me, honey—any time.'

Vara had turned. He was frowning, but he said nothing. Juanita went into the bedroom. The others began to eat.

*   *   *

Someone tapped lightly on the door. They had heard no one approaching, and instantly they all stopped eating and stared at the door, as though by doing so it might have been possible to see who was standing on the other side. For a few moments there was silence, broken only by the sound of traffic moving along the Avenida Almirante Diaz.

Then Albores said softly: 'You had better see who it is, Mark.'

'It could be the police.'

'Nevertheless, you had better open the door.'

'Before they kick it down,' McCall said.

Aston crossed the room and pulled the door open. Peters was standing outside.

'Hello, Mark,' he said; and then he looked past Aston's shoulder and saw the others. 'Oh, I'm sorry. I didn't know you had visitors.'

Aston was undecided whether or not to invite Peters in. But he could hardly leave the man standing on the threshold, so finally he said: 'Won't you come in?'

Peters stepped into the room and Aston closed the door. Peters was wearing his informal clothes—tan slacks, a blazer and suede shoes; from which one could have deduced that it was a holiday even without previous knowledge of the fact. Albores, McCall and Vara were all staring at him as though at some unusual kind of animal. It seemed to embarrass him.

'Why don't you introduce us, Mark?' Albores said smoothly; and he smiled at Peters, friendly, relaxed.

Aston made the introduction. Peters seemed to be wondering whether or not to shake hands with the young men; but none of them made any move in that direction and he let his own half-raised hand fall to his side.

'These are all Juanita's friends,' Aston explained.

'Ah, I see,' Peters said, as though suddenly enlightened. 'And Miss Merengo herself? She is well?'

At that moment the girl came out of the bedroom. She had dressed herself in jeans and a check shirt, and she must have heard Aston introducing Peters, for she showed no surprise at seeing him.

'Why, Mr. Peters. How nice to see you. How is Eva?'

'She is well. She often speaks of you. We must get together again some evening.'

'That would be nice.'

Peters turned to Aston. 'Actually it was Eva's idea that I should call. She—that is, we—have a small favour to ask of you.'

'Yes?'

'Eva has decided that she would like to watch the procession this afternoon.'

'Yes?' Aston said again. He had a premonition of what was coming.

Peters gave a nervous cough. 'Well, as you know, our house is well away from the route and it's pretty chaotic in the streets; you get terribly jostled and there's no guarantee that you'll be able to see much anyway. So we thought you might let us have a seat at your window.'

Aston was silent. No one else spoke. The request seemed to hang in the warm air of the room like a threat.

Peters coughed again. He glanced at the three young men, discovered that they were all staring at him, and glanced hurriedly away.

'Of course if it's not convenient— '

117

'It's a question of space,' Aston said.

'Space?'

'One window. Five people already.'

'You mean you are all going to watch the procession?'

'It is why we are here,' Albores said. 'We would not miss it for the world.'

'Eva will be disappointed,' Peters said. 'I'm afraid we rather took it for granted. But of course—in the circumstances—'

'I'm sorry,' Aston said; but the thought had leapt into his mind that here might be a way out. If he were to allow Peters and his wife to join the party, the assassination would be off; nothing could be done while they were in the room. And what could Albores and the others do about it? Nothing.

'May I?' Peters said. He crossed the room and looked out on to the Avenida Almirante Din. 'It is a large window. Perhaps there would be space for all. Three on chairs in front, the rest standing behind.' He turned. 'Don't you think so?'

It was Juanita who answered. 'It would be too much of a crush. Those at the back would have difficulty in seeing clearly.'

Peters was obviously dismayed by opposition coming from this quarter. Possibly he had expected the girl to be more obliging and was making a rapid readjustment in his opinion of her.

He said a little stiffly: 'Well, it's up to you.

118

But I should have thought it would not have been too difficult to fit in just two more.'

'It's always the two more that make the difference. There is a proverb, isn't there, about the last straw and the camel's back.' She was smiling, but Aston saw that she knew very well what she was doing. Peters was a man who had a keen sense of his own dignity and it was not difficult to offend him. He was being offended now. 'I really am afraid you and Eva will have to look somewhere else. Of course, if only you had asked soon enough, I am sure Mark and I would have been happy to oblige; but you are a little late, aren't you?'

'Yes,' Peters said, and he had gone rather red in the face, 'I see that I am. Well, in that case I'll not intrude any further.' He walked to the door, turned, gave a curt, jerky nod to Juanita and the three young men, and went out of the room, carrying an invisible cloud of injury with him.

Aston followed him out on to the landing and closed the door behind him. 'I'm sorry about that, but you see how it is.'

Peters looked at him with a severe and disapproving expression on his face. 'Yes, I do see how it is.'

'It would have been rather crowded, and Eva might not have liked that.'

'She might not have liked the company—certainly. So those are Miss Merengo's friends.'

'You don't approve of them?'

'They don't strike me as being the kind of people I should care to associate with, and I would advise you to be very careful. Quite frankly, they look like trouble-makers to me.'

'You really think so?'

'I do. It wouldn't surprise me in the least to learn that they all belong to one of these revolutionary groups—urban guerrillas or the like.'

'In that case it's perhaps as well you're not coming back this afternoon. They might decide to kidnap you.'

'It is no laughing matter,' Peters said huffily. 'I'm sorry to say I may find it necessary to change my opinion regarding Miss Merengo. It's a great pity when an attractive and charming girl gets mixed up in things like that.'

'You don't know she's mixed up in anything.'

'I'm going by instinct, and my instinct tells me that those men are a bad lot. In my opinion you'd do well to have no more to do with them.'

Aston had an impulse to confide in Peters; to ask for Peters's advice. But he knew what that advice would be: go at once to the police and make a full statement. And of course it was impossible to go to the police because of Juanita. Moreover, if he breathed a word of what was afoot to Peters, the man would blow the whole thing without a moment's hesitation,

Juanita or no Juanita. He would feel it his duty to do so; and the devil of it was, he would be right.

'Well,' Aston said, 'maybe I'll do as you say. And I'm sorry about the window. I hope Eva won't be too put out about it.'

Peters made a little fluttering gesture with his hand. 'It's not important. We'll make other arrangements. But don't forget what I've said, will you? I'd hate to see you get into trouble.' He sounded genuinely concerned, and Aston regretted that it was so utterly impossible to confide in him. Peters was not such a bad sort really.

'I won't forget,' he said; and then it occurred to him that this could well be the last time he ever saw Peters, and he held out his hand. 'Good-bye.'

Peters seemed surprised, but he shook hands. It must have struck him, however, that this appeared rather like a long farewell, for he said: 'I'll see you at the office tomorrow, of course. Work as usual tomorrow, eh?'

'Of course,' Aston said; and he watched Peters walk to the stairs and go down with one hand on the banister rail, careful as ever. In a way, he was sorry to see him go; it was like the end of something; a chapter of his life perhaps. He turned and went back into the apartment.

They all looked at him, and he could see that they were suspicious—even Juanita.

'That took a long time,' Vara said. 'What

121

were you doing?'

'Talking.'

'What were you talking about?'

'Is that any of your business?'

'It could be,' Vara said. 'It could be very much our business. You were not maybe telling him why he couldn't watch the procession from this window?'

'He already knew why. Juanita told him.'

'But she didn't tell him the real reason, and maybe you did.'

'Don't you trust me, Eduardo?' He looked at Vara and then at the others, smiling a little. Let them worry; they had given him enough worries. 'Don't any of you trust me?'

'Why should we trust you?' Vara said.

'I don't know. I don't know any reason why you should. But you have to, don't you?'

'We don't have to.'

'No? Well, let's suppose you decide not to. Suppose you come to the conclusion that I told Mr. Peters all about what you intend to do and that he's right now on his way to the police, what can you do about it?'

No one answered. Their eyes were fixed on him, as though each were trying to see into his mind and read the truth that was printed there.

He gave a laugh, though he had seldom felt less inclined to laughter. 'I'll tell you what you can do. You can call the whole thing off and get to hell out of here before the alarm bells

122

start ringing.'

Still they were silent, staring at him.

Then Albores said softly: 'You would like us to do that, wouldn't you, Mark? You would like it very much.'

'You bet I would.'

Albores shook his head. 'But we will not do it.'

'You're going to wait for Peters to call the police?'

'He will not call the police, because you did not tell him.'

'You're sure of that?'

'I am sure. There are reasons why you would not tell him. At least, there is one reason.'

Albores was shrewd.

Aston crossed to the table and took a sandwich. He did not feel hungry, he was too nervous, but it might be well to eat something. The food stuck in his throat and he had to swill it down with beer.

He looked at his watch. Two hours and a quarter to go.

*   *   *

'I think you had better go to the car, Eduardo,' Albores said.

'There is time.'

'There is time, but it would be better if you went now.' Albores turned to Aston. 'Your bag

123

is ready?'

'Yes.'

'Fetch it. Eduardo will take it to the car.'

'And Juanita's?'

'Hers also.'

Aston went into the bedroom and fetched the two duffle-bags. Vara took them without a word and left the apartment.

'I think Juanita should go too,' Aston said.

Albores disagreed. 'We must have the window occupied; it might arouse suspicion otherwise.'

'Two of us would be enough.'

'A woman also would make it seem more natural.'

'I still think she should go. It would be safer.'

'I will stay,' the girl said.

Aston shrugged resignedly. 'That settles it then.'

He walked again to the window and looked out. There was more activity below; crowds were already gathering; people were staking out their claims on the pavement. It was a very colourful scene, with everyone dressed up for the occasion: women in gay dresses; children waving cheap flags; sunlight glinting on earrings and bracelets, on the helmets and the rifles of the soldiers lining the route. A hum, as of a vast swarm of bees, rose in the hot afternoon air, an amorphous mass of sound, drifting like smoke.

These people, Aston reflected, did not look depressed, down-trodden, ripe for rebellion, for revolution. But the outward show on a national holiday might be misleading; deep down inside them a fire might be smouldering, needing only a touch, a breath, to make it leap into flame. And might not that touch, that breath, be perhaps a bullet aimed from a window?

He saw a jeep come to a halt. Four policemen got out, pushed through the crowd and walked towards the house. He turned and saw that McCall had rolled back the carpet, had lifted the floor-board and was taking the rifle from its hiding-place.

He said: 'You'd better put that back. The police are coming.'

McCall asked no questions. He pushed the rifle back into the cavity, replaced the board and pulled the carpet over it. They could hear the heavy tread of boots on the stairs.

'So,' McCall said, 'maybe you did tell Peters.'

'No.'

'Why would they come to this house now?'

'A last-minute check-up.'

'It could be,' Albores said. 'We shall see. Sit down and relax.'

McCall sat down. Albores did so too. Juanita picked up some empty beer glasses and carried them to the kitchen. Aston remained standing by the window.

125

The door was flung open without any ceremony and the same two policemen who had searched the apartment the previous day walked in.

'Well, do come in,' Aston said. 'You want another glass of beer?'

'There is not time,' the bony policeman said. His gaze flickered round the room, missing nothing. 'Who are these?' He indicated Albores and McCall.

'Friends who have come to watch the procession from my window.'

'Names.'

They told him. He demanded proof of their identity, and they gave him proof. He stared hard at McCall.

'Why are you in Mendoza?'

'I like it here.'

'You have work?'

'I am looking for work.'

'What kind of work?'

'Engineering.'

'Ah!'

The younger policeman was moving about restlessly. He came to a stop where the loose board was. He kept testing it with his foot, producing a creaking sound. Aston would not have been surprised if he had decided to pull it up and search again beneath the floor. And this time he might find the rifle.

Then Juanita came in from the kitchen, and he stopped treading on the board and stared at her, eyes smouldering.

'Ah, señorita,' the bony policeman said. 'So you are still here.'

'I am still here.'

'You too intend to watch the procession?'

'Yes.'

'You will have a good view from here.' He crossed to the window and peered out, shifting from one position to another, as though to test every angle. He came back and spoke again to McCall. 'You have been in the United States Army perhaps?'

'Yes,' McCall said.

'And you can handle a rifle?'

'If necessary. If there is one to handle.'

'You would not say that it was necessary today, for example?'

'For what purpose?' McCall asked, meeting the policeman's gaze coolly.

The policeman stroked his beak of a nose with one bony finger. 'Let us say, for example, in order to shoot a president.'

McCall laughed. 'You're speaking to the wrong guy. I've done my killing. All I want now is a peaceful life. No more guns, no more bombs, no more rockets. Never.'

He was putting on a good act. Aston would have been convinced if he had not known it was an act. The policeman again looked out of the window.

'It is certainly a fine view.'

'Perhaps you would like to stay and watch

127

the procession,' Aston said.

The policeman seemed to detect no irony in the suggestion. He shook his head. 'Unfortunately, there are duties to perform.' He spoke to the other man. 'Search the bedroom, I will look in the other rooms.'

It did not take long. They found nothing suspicious. It was perhaps as well that Vara had taken the bags; such obvious signs of preparations for departure might have appeared odd. The younger policeman returned to the loose board beneath the carpet as though drawn irresistibly to it. He again tested it with his foot, producing that same creaking sound.

'Perhaps,' he said, 'we should look under the floor again.'

'For more dead rats?' the older man said. 'There is not time. We will go now.'

The younger policeman did not like it. Aston guessed that he was still smarting from his humiliation of the day before and would have liked to find something incriminating enough to warrant an arrest. But he did not argue; he followed the bony policeman out of the apartment and Aston closed the door.

'I think you should lock it this time,' Albores said.

Aston did so.

Juanita said: 'They are leaving the house now.' She had moved to the window. 'They will surely not come again.'

'It is unlikely,' Albores agreed. He glanced at his watch. 'Time is slipping away. You had better get the rifle now, Red.'

Aston sighed. Nothing was going to stop it now. Peters, the police, had come and gone without affecting the issue. Now it seemed inevitable. Perhaps it had been fated.

He watched McCall assembling the rifle.

CHAPTER TEN

SHOOTING INCIDENT

They sat in the open window with their hands resting on the sill. Albores was on the left, then Juanita, then Aston. On Aston's right, seated on a chair and concealed by the folds of the curtain, was McCall with the rifle. McCall could not be seen from outside, but he could see out through a narrow gap between the curtain and the window-frame. The barrel of the rifle rested on the sill, inconspicuous, even invisible from below.

The crowd had thickened; it filled the pavements on each side of the Avenida Almirante Diaz and pressed against the restraining rows of soldiers. Here and there it bulged like a bow until pressed back into place; then the bulge would appear at some other point, and then at another, as though some vast ripple were passing along the line.

Aston gazed across the avenue and saw the child on the balcony on the other side. She had been joined by a man and a woman, probably her parents; she kept glancing up at one or other of them, saying something and then gazing again up the Avenida Almirante Diaz in impatient expectation of the procession that must soon appear. The small flag was still in her hand, and from time to time she waved it vigorously, as though by doing so she might have speeded up the proceedings.

'They are coming,' Juanita said, a catch of excitement in her voice.

Aston turned his head. Away to the left the motor-cycle escort had come into view, the white crash-helmets and white gloves of the police riders picked out by the sunlight, the chromium plating of the machines glittering like silver. Behind the escort came the blue and gold car of the President, a big open Cadillac with the flag of the Republic on one wing and the Stars and Stripes on the other. At that distance it was not yet possible to recognise the figures sitting in the car, but McCall had probably already picked up his target in the telescopic sight on his rifle. The noise of the crowd grew in intensity, rising like a solid block to strike the eardrums.

'Yes, they are coming,' Albores said. He sounded calm; but surely, Aston thought, his heart must be pumping too, his pulse

130

throbbing madly.

He repeated Albores's words softly, scarcely audibly: 'Yes, they are coming.' And he could feel the sweat breaking out on his forehead and collecting under his armpits. His stomach was fluttering and the bones seemed to have melted in his limbs. The roar of the crowd came like the surge of waves on a seashore, rising and falling, pounding at his senses until he felt that he must faint from the heat and the noise and the consciousness of approaching, unavoidable tragedy.

He heard the creak of McCall's chair, and the small tube of grey metal that was the barrel of the rifle shifted slightly on the window-sill, following its target as tenaciously as a stoat following a rabbit. How could anyone, Aston wondered, kill like this in cold blood? He could not understand the mentality of such a man. Yet was he not as bad as McCall, since he was allowing it to happen? Were they not all as bad? The girl too. To take a man's life—and for what? A cause which it could not help. It was madness. And with McCall it was not even a cause that was impelling him; it was a kind of vengeance; he was avenging himself for something he had lost in the bloodstained paddy-fields of Vietnam, in the jungles and villages of Indo-China. And that something? Innocence perhaps, a belief in the essential decency of mankind; belief, above all, in his own decency, his own morality.

So there they were, the four of them, waiting to kill the Vice-President of the United States: Albores and Juanita because of a blind faith, a blind hope that this act of assassination might somehow benefit the people of their country; McCall to serve his private ends, his private feud with the American Government; and he, Mark Aston, because of a passion, a desire, that he could not resist. Perhaps he was the guiltiest of them all.

Behind the President's car were other official cars, a military band, and then, just coming into view, the decorated the Republic—industry, agriculture, sport, education, entertainment, arts and crafts, and so on. Aston knew that he would never have a chance to see them clearly; before ever they came near enough the shot would be fired and anarchy would take over. Out of the corner of his eye he again caught sight of the child in the red and white dress; she was dancing up and down on the balcony and waving the flag in her hand.

Again the rifle barrel shifted a little on the sill.

He wondered where Peters and Eva were. Perhaps they had gone to the Plaza Lopez, which was where the procession was heading. There the President of the Republic and the Vice-President of the United States would each place a wreath on the monument to Pedro Lopez, the Scorpion, and then would

132

make brief speeches before proceeding to the Presidential Residence for a garden party and other celebrations. But, of course, the Vice-President would never get to the garden party; he would never lay a wreath on the monument or make his speech in the Plaza Lopez; because he would be dead.

Aston noticed that something was happening below; the pressure of the crowd had apparently been too heavy for the soldiers and a gap had been opened in the line. Through this gap, like water flooding through a breach in a dike, people were flowing on to the avenue in an ever increasing mass. It was impossible for the motor-cycle escort to force a way through, and they came to a halt. The President's car halted also, and the motor-cyclists fell back to form a screen around it, protecting it from the encroaching flood of humanity. Behind the President's car the entire procession ground to a standstill, stretching far up the Avenida Almirante Diaz like a multi-coloured ribbon.

Albores swore. This was something he had not foreseen. The blue and gold Cadillac was a hundred yards away; it was no range at all if McCall could get a line on his target. But the Vice-President was sitting down, and even if there had been no crowd milling round the car there would still have been a screen of toughened glass between him and the rifle. The plan had been to wait until the car was

133

almost level with the window, when the screen would no longer offer any protection, and then fire down into it.

'What do we do now?' Juanita asked. She sounded nervous.

'Wait,' Albores said. 'They will clear a way through.'

But with such a solid block of people barring the way, it seemed probable that any operation on those lines would inevitably take a deal of time. For the present at least everything had come to a standstill.

Aston wiped the sweat from his hands and his mouth felt parched.

'What do you think, Red?' Albores said. 'What is the chance of taking him now?'

'It'd be a risk,' McCall said. 'I might do it, but it'd be a hell of a risk. There wouldn't be a second chance; he'd be down on the floor of the car before you could think.'

'Better not try it then. Not yet.'

'Oh, God!' the girl said. 'More waiting.'

Aston could understand how she felt. They had been keyed up; the moment had almost arrived, the moment of release from tension; and now this.

'Patience,' Albores said. 'We can wait a little longer. It will make no difference.'

They waited. Five minutes passed. Nothing had happened, except that the crowd had become more uncontrolled, more vociferous. Some people were shouting slogans which were not altogether flattering to President Figueiras, and it occurred to Aston that the stoppage might not have been altogether unplanned. A few placards had appeared and the thing seemed to be taking more and more the appearance of a political demonstration.

And then, incredibly, the Vice-President stood up. He seemed to be trying to see what was going on, and he stood there in his pale grey suit like a sentinel, turning his head first one way and then another. He could not have presented a better target if that had been his sole object.

'Now,' Albores breathed. 'You can take him now.'

Aston, too, was standing up. He was looking at McCall. McCall had his eye to the telescopic sight and the butt of the rifle was pressed against his shoulder. The forefinger of his right hand was curled about the trigger.

'No,' Aston said. It was scarcely more than a whisper.

McCall made no sign of having heard. Perhaps he was too engrossed in the task he had to do for any words to reach his brain.

'No,' Aston said again, louder this time.

He heard a movement on his left; Albores and Juanita were also standing up. The rifle was steady in McCall's hands and his attention had not wavered for an instant. Aston sensed that the moment had come, that he was about to squeeze the trigger and end a man's life.

It was an action taken without conscious thought, an instinctive gesture that should repudiate the whole sickening business, a last-minute drawing back from the very brink of the abyss. He leaned across, grasped the stock of the rifle with his right hand, and wrenched it away from McCall's shoulder; downward and towards him in a single rapid movement.

He heard McCall's shout of anger blending with the crack of the gun. The butt, in recoil, struck McCall hard on the chest, and Juanita gave a kind of sobbing cry of dismay. She was staring with horrified eyes at the house on the other side of the Avenida Almirante Diaz, the house where the child had been waving a flag.

'Oh, God, no!'

Aston followed the direction of her gaze and could not see the child; only the man and the woman bending down towards something lying on the floor of the balcony. He could not believe it; he did not wish to believe it; and yet he had to. He saw the flag; it was on the balcony, poking out through the wrought-iron railings. For a moment it hung there, balanced; then it tilted over the edge and fell like a shot bird, fluttering, to the ground.

He stood there, staring stupidly. Below him the crowd seemed unaware of what had happened. The Vice-President had sat down and was leaning over to speak to the President.

'You son-of-a-bitch,' McCall said. 'You goddamn lousy son-of-a-stinking-bitch.'

136

Aston caught a glimpse of the rifle in McCall's hands, the butt moving in a tight arc. It struck him a bone-jarring blow on the left-hand side of the jaw, and he fell sideways, landing heavily on his right shoulder, feeling sick and hurt, but still remembering the child and the awful blankness of that gap where she had stood and danced and waved to him.

He made no attempt to get up. Things had drifted out of focus; he was seeing the room through a kind of mist. Voices came to him as if deadened by layers of cotton-wool.

Albores was speaking. 'We'd better go. There's nothing we can do now. We must get away.' Incredibly, he still sounded calm.

'And that bastard?'

'Leave him.'

'I'd like to put a bullet in his lousy carcase.'

'What good would it do? Let's go.'

Juanita's voice broke in then. 'We can't leave him here. We can't just run away and leave him to the police.'

'I can,' McCall said.

His head was beginning to clear; the focus was hardening. He saw that they had all drawn away from the window, that McCall was still holding the rifle.

'We must take him with us,' the girl said. She seemed to be appealing to Albores. 'We owe it to him.'

'We owe him nothing now,' Albores said.

'It was an accident.'

'Christ!' McCall said. 'Some accident!'

He was raising himself off the floor now; he was on his hands and knees, head drooping, trying to control the sickness, afraid that he might vomit.

Albores moved towards the door. 'Are you coming?'

'Not without Mark,' Juanita said.

He heard his own voice then, croaking. 'You'd better go. I'm no use to you any more. Leave me.'

The noise of the crowd came in through the window. Was it his imagination or was there a sullen note of anger in it? Had the people become aware of the shooting of the child?

He felt someone tugging at his arm. 'Get up, Mark. You must get up.'

He was on his feet then, not entirely steady, teetering a little; but the girl's hand was supporting him. Albores was at the door; he had unlocked but had not opened it. He was looking back at them. McCall was a couple of yards away, and he seemed ready to take another swipe with the rifle. He had some cause to feel resentful. They all had.

'Juanita,' Albores said. He was pleading now.

'Not without Mark,' she repeated.

Albores gave a shrug of resignation. 'Very well; but let us go now.'

'You're taking him along?' McCall sounded disbelieving.

138

'There is no time for argument. Leave the gun.'

'No. I'm taking it.'

'Are you crazy? How far would you get with that? Do you imagine you can shoot your way out of this?'

'Maybe you're right.' McCall threw the rifle on to the settee and walked to the door, ignoring Aston.

Albores opened the door and peered out. He signalled that it was all clear. He and McCall went out on to the landing.

'Come, Mark,' Juanita said.

'But the child—'

'You can do nothing about the child.'

It was the bare truth. It was the truth he would have to live with. He followed her out of the apartment and closed the door carefully behind him. He wished he could as easily have closed off from his mind the events of the past few minutes.

They went out by the back of the house, having met no one. There was a neglected garden ending at a wooden fence. A gate in the fence gave access to a tarmac foot-path. They turned right and a brief, rapid walk brought them to a road running at right angles to the Avenida Almirante Diaz.

It was a very quiet road; there were a few cars parked at the kerbside, but there was no traffic moving. It was the Feast of the Scorpion and no doubt everyone had gone to watch the procession. The houses on each side looked lifeless, abandoned, drowsing in the heat.

McCall glanced up and down the road. 'Where in hell's Eddie? He should be here. He should be waiting. Where in hell is he?'

Albores did not answer the question. He just said: 'Let's start walking.'

They began to walk away from the Avenida Almirante Diaz, and they had taken no more than a dozen paces when a jeep came out of a side-turning and drove slowly towards them. It was a police jeep and there was one man in it. He pulled it to a halt by the kerb, got out, and stood in the middle of the road—waiting for them. It was the younger of the two policemen who had searched the apartment, the one who had a grudge. He was holding a sub-machine-gun; not pointing it at them, just holding it ready.

'Keep walking,' Albores said. 'Don't hurry it.'

Aston wanted to run, but he knew that Albores was right. Start running, and the gun would get to work; it was all that was needed to set it off. He wondered whether the policeman knew about the shooting incident, but he doubted it; he had probably simply been patrolling in the jeep, keeping an eye open for anything suspicious. And he had undoubtedly found something suspicious.

He allowed them to approach to within ten paces of him before ordering them to stop.

They did so, Albores and McCall in front, Aston and the girl a short distance behind.

'You are going somewhere?' the policeman said.

It was Albores who answered. 'Yes.'

'You are tired of watching the parade?'

They could hear the muffled roar of the crowd coming from the Avenida Almirante Diaz, and faint strains of music, indicating that the military band was still valiantly performing in spite of the hold-up. Perhaps the news of the shooting had not reached back along the line; perhaps even the President knew nothing about it. But soon it would be common knowledge; soon the police would be searching for the weapon. And when they had found it they would know whom they had to pursue. It was no time to be standing there talking.

'Yes,' Albores said, 'we are tired of watching.'

'So you decide to take a walk, eh?' There was suspicion in the policeman's eyes, in his voice, in his expression, in the very way he stood there. He had sensed that something was not as it should have been.

'Is there anything illegal in taking a walk?' Albores asked.

'Illegal? No. But it is curious. You were not perhaps running away from something?'

'We were not running.'

'True.'

'So now may we go on our way?'

141

'You are in a hurry then?'

'I did not say that.'

'So you are not in a hurry but you do not wish to stay here?' The policeman was taunting them. It could have been that he was uncertain what to do and was trying to make up his mind. He had no reason for holding them, but there was that grudge, that humiliation. He was reluctant to let them go.

Aston glanced back the way they had come. There was no sign of pursuit—yet; but time was precious and it was slipping away.

McCall's patience cracked. 'Let's go.' He took a step forward and the sub-machine-gun swung to cover him. 'Stop!'

McCall stopped; he had no wish to commit suicide. 'I think,' the policeman said, 'we will go back to your apartment, Señor Aston. All of us.'

'Why?' Albores asked.

'Perhaps we shall discover that when we get there.'

'But—'

'Do not argue.' The gun moved in his hands, menacing. 'Turn around.'

Aston was about to turn when he saw the car coming. It was a big Ford that had done a lot of service and was not as smart as it had once been. The red paintwork was dull and scratched, and there were some dents here and there and bits of rust that nobody seemed to be bothering about any more. Not that he

142

noticed all the details just then; all he noticed was that the car was coming fast and that the policeman was standing in the middle of the road with his back to it. The driver must have seen him, but the speed of the big Ford did not slacken; if anything, it appeared to increase, as though the driver had slammed his foot down on the accelerator.

The policeman, with his mind on other things, seemed to be unaware of the danger; he was still snarling orders at the four on the pavement, yelling at them to turn around and start walking. But then something in their attitudes, in the way they were all staring past him up the road, must have warned him of his peril. Or it might have been that he had at last heard the car approaching.

There would have been time even then. If he had leapt either to his left or his right he could have saved himself. It did not seem to occur to him. As he turned to face it, the car was just twenty feet away; he raised the sub-machine-gun to fire at it, and the front bumper hit him in the legs and the gun flew out of his hands and landed at the side of the road with a metallic clatter. For perhaps five seconds he seemed to be glued to the front of the car; then he fell back and it went over him.

Aston heard the screech of tyres as the car was braked hard and pulled to a stop. It made a quick turn and came back. The policeman was still lying in the road and it went over him again and stopped where the four were standing. Vara was behind the wheel.

'Get in! Hurry!'

McCall made a move towards the sub-machine-gun. 'Leave it!' Albores said.

McCall left it. They got into the car and slammed the doors. Albores was in front; Aston and McCall were in the back with the girl between them. Aston could feel her shuddering. Vara let the clutch in and accelerated hard.

'You were late,' Albores said.

CHAPTER ELEVEN

NO FOUL PLAY

There were no road blocks. It was evident that neither the shooting of the girl nor the running down of the police-man had yet started a full-scale manhunt. And with so many of the police occupied with security measures along the route of the procession, it might be some time before concerted action could be taken.

They were clear of the suburbs and heading away from the town before any of them talked much. Then Vara said:

'Did it go?'

'No,' Albores said. 'It all went wrong.'

'You mean Red missed?'

144

'He missed.'

'And he was supposed to be the marksman.' There was utter disgust in Vara's voice. 'He's the marksman and he misses the target. Santa Maria!'

'Hold it,' McCall said.

'Mark jogged his arm,' Albores explained. 'The bullet hit a kid. Maybe the kid's dead. We don't know.'

Vara stood on the brake so hard they were all thrown forward with the jolt.

'What are you doing?' Albores demanded.

'Stopping the car.'

He must have taken some of the tread off the tyres, the way he had used the brakes. The car skidded to a halt, and Vara turned in his seat and looked at Aston.

'Why did you do that?'

'Do what?'

'Jog his arm.'

'I didn't jog his arm; I grabbed the rifle. And I did it to stop him shooting the Vice-President.'

'You preferred to have him shoot a child?'

'Don't be a damned fool. I didn't mean that to happen.'

'But it did?'

'Yes, it did.'

'So you saved the Vice-President and you got a child shot. You feel good about that?'

'Of course I don't feel good about it.' Aston was beginning to shout, not sorry to relieve his feelings by snarling at Vara. 'If you want to know, I feel sick. I feel sick and dirty, and I doubt whether I'm ever going to feel clean again as long as I live, because there'll always be that child in my mind—always. So don't talk to me, Eddie; just don't bloody talk to me.'

'Get out,' Vara said. His voice was cold and hard.

'No,' Juanita said. ' He comes with us.'

'I don't drive the car with him in it.'

'Maybe you'd like me to drive,' Aston said. His jaw felt bad where McCall had hit it with the rifle; it was swelling and it hurt him to move it; but perhaps he was lucky it had not been broken.

'We ought to kill him,' Vara said. 'Everything we planned, and he had to wreck it. I knew we should never have trusted him.'

'You had to trust me. You couldn't do anything else.'

'For Pete's sake,' McCall said, 'get the car moving. You want us to be picked up?'

An ancient lorry hammered past, heading in the direction of Mendoza and raising a cloud of dust.

'We drop him first.'

'If we drop him here,' Albores said, 'he could help the police get on our trail. We'll talk about it later, but now do what Red says.'

Vara allowed himself to be persuaded. He got the car going again and seemed to be trying to work off his anger by driving like a

146

madman. He overtook a white Volkswagen and narrowly avoided a head-on collision with an oil-tanker coming in the opposite direction. No one said anything; if his driving had been criticised it would probably have made him even madder.

A little later Albores said: 'You know where we turn off?'

'I know,' Vara said testily. 'It's another two kilometres before we get to the turning. Let me do the driving.'

The road had been climbing steadily and its surface had deteriorated abruptly once they had cleared the outskirts of the town. The road they got on to when Vara took the turning off to the right was, however, far worse; it was not metalled and it was full of ruts and pot-holes. Vara was forced to reduce his speed, but even so the car bumped and swayed, throwing the occupants from side to side. It was a twisting road, winding between rocks and hills in its gradual descent. It seemed to Aston that they were to some extent doubling back on their tracks, for they were certainly heading again towards the coast. He thought of asking what the plan was, but decided that it would probably be a waste of breath. And if he drew attention to himself they might, after all, change their minds and throw him out; which in that kind of country was not at all an attractive prospect.

They encountered no traffic except a man

with a couple of pack-mules travelling in the opposite direction. He gave them scarcely a glance, but Albores swore.

'What's wrong?' McCall asked.

'That man.'

'What about him? He looked half asleep.'

'Possibly. On the other hand he may remember this car. I think that cars are not too plentiful on this road.'

'So he remembers. So what?'

'So he could tell the police.'

'You worry too much,' McCall said. But he sounded a little worried himself.

A mile or so further on Vara made another sharp turn and brought them on to an even worse road, a mere track that looked as though it was hardly ever used. It passed through a narrow gorge with steep sides on which grew a few scrubby bushes and some sparse, tough-looking grass. At the other end of the gorge they came to a kind of rocky arena surrounded by hills which appeared to be the site of some old mine workings, long since abandoned and derelict.

A couple of dilapidated huts stood on one side close up against a cliff, like people huddled there for shelter; and there were some rusting rails and a few empty trams standing in a row, as though waiting for the miners who would never return.

Vara brought the car to a halt, and no one moved or spoke for a moment or two, just

148

sitting there in silence and maybe thinking about their future. Then Albores opened the door on his side and got out. McCall followed suit.

'Is this the end of the ride?' Aston asked.

'It should have been the end for you a long way back,' Vara said. His temper did not appear to have improved at all.

'You had better get out, Mark,' Juanita said.

He did so, and the girl followed him.

Vara had also got out. He walked round to the front of the car and examined it.

'Look at this,' he said.

The others looked. There were a lot of dents and scratches, but they had been there before and Vara was not calling attention to them. There was something else, something that was of more recent date. It looked as though someone might have shaken some paint off a brush while standing near the car, so that the paint had splashed on the radiator grille, spattering across it in the shape of a fan. But they all knew it was not paint. There was some of it on the bumper too, dark and clotted. Albores stooped and pulled something out of a crack in the wing where it had been wedged. It looked like a piece of black wool with a strip of skin attached to it. Aston remembered that the policeman's hair had been black and had curled like wool.

The colour seemed to drain from the girl's face. She turned and walked away, stumbling a little, as though moving in the dark. She was making retching sounds.

'I think the guy's dead,' McCall said.

Vara said savagely: 'Of course he's dead. But we should have stopped and cleaned this off. Driving all that way like this. Suppose we'd run into some police.'

'You ran into one,' McCall said.

'You think that's funny?'

'I don't think anything's funny. You were driving. Why didn't you see to it?'

'I couldn't see it from inside the car. You others should have noticed it before you got in.'

'You think that was the time to go round looking for bits of hair and blood? All we wanted was out of there—and fast.'

'Well, let's not argue about it,' Albores said. 'We were lucky. But that kind of luck may not hold. Let's get the luggage out of the car.'

He opened the boot and started unloading. There were some bottles of Coca-Cola and a polythene bag as well as the kit. Aston picked up his own duffle-bag and Juanita's and walked to where she was standing with her back to the car. She looked sick.

'Are you feeling ill?' he asked.

She answered in a low voice, barely above a whisper: 'It's horrible. I did not think it would be like this.'

He believed her. The shooting of a politician from a distance was one thing: you

150

did not touch him, did not even see the wound or hear the cry of pain; it was just an operation—clean, impersonal, hygienic. But to have a man's blood spattered over your car; that was something else, something closer and more savage: it was the dirt showing through the fabric of the ideal.

'Perhaps it's always like this,' he said. 'In the end.'

Albores came up then, carrying more of the kit. 'Let us go inside. Come.'

He led the way to the smaller of the two huts. The hinges squealed as he pushed the door open. He went in. The others followed.

It seemed gloomy after the bright sunlight outside. There was only one window, most of the glass broken, and the shadow of the cliff lay on the hut. There was a strong, musty odour of disuse and there were cobwebs everywhere. A wooden bench against the far wall and a rough table constituted the only furniture, and the floor was rotting.

McCall was carrying the bottles; he put them on the table and Albores set down the polythene bag beside them. They dumped the kit on the floor.

Albores spoke to Vara. 'Better get the car out of sight. I'll come with you. Maybe you'd better come too, Red.'

'Do you want me?' Aston asked.

'No,' Albores said. 'You stay here.'

The three went out of the hut.

'Where are they going to hide the car?' Aston asked.

The girl replied briefly, as though the answer were obvious: 'In the mine.'

'And it takes three of them to do that?'

'Perhaps they intend to clean it. And, of course, there are the guns to fetch.'

'What guns?'

'The guns that are hidden in the mine.'

'You stowed them away in there?'

'Naturally.'

'Why?'

'Because they might be needed.'

'Well, that's fine,' Aston said. 'That really is fine.'

He walked to the window and looked out. Vara was just starting the car; Albores and McCall had not bothered to get in. About fifty yards away was an excavation in the hillside like the entrance to a cave; it was one of the old mine workings. Vara drove the car towards the opening, bumping over loose rocks and other obstacles; it went into the tunnel with room to spare and disappeared from sight. Albores and McCall walked in after it.

Aston turned away from the window and saw that the girl was sitting on the bench. She still looked pretty sick. He moved across the hut and sat down beside her. After a while Albores and McCall came back. Albores was carrying three Colt .45 automatics, McCall had two 9 millimetre Lugers and some boxes of ammunition. They put everything on the table. It seemed a lot of hardware.

'Have you ever used a pistol, Mark?' Albores asked.

'No,' Aston said.

'It's simple. I'll show you.'

'I don't want to use one.'

'You'd rather let the police take you?'

'I thought we weren't having any more trouble with the police. I thought from here on it was all to go as smoothly as a jug of cream.'

'One should always be prepared for the worst.'

'I'd never hit anything with one of those.'

'You could scare people.'

'I could scare myself.'

Vara came in. He was carrying a small transistor radio and an electric torch, the rubber-cased kind. He put them on the table with the other things. It was beginning to look like a stall at a jumble sale—except that jumble sales seldom handled anything quite as lethal as Colts and Lugers.

Vara seemed to be still on the boil. 'So it comes to this,' he said bitterly. 'After all the planning and scheming, after all the work, after all the waiting, it comes to this.'

'It will not help to moan about it,' Albores told him. 'We have to go on from here.'

Vara looked at Aston with hatred. 'Why don't we kill him now? What have we to lose?'

'And what would we gain from doing so?'

153

'Satisfaction. He is to blame for our failure.'

'Why don't you give the real reason why you'd like to kill me?' Aston said. 'The reason why you hate me.'

Albores glanced at him. 'What real reason?'

'Jealousy.'

'Jealousy?'

'Are you blind? Can't you see he wants Juanita for himself? That's why he'd be glad to get rid of me. It galls him to know she prefers me to him.'

He had not been aware that Vara carried a knife. It must have been concealed somewhere about his person, for suddenly it was in his hand and he was coming in to attack like a madman. But McCall was too quick for him; he stuck out a long leg and tripped Vara. Vara went down with a crash but he kept his grip on the knife; it had a bone handle and a thin, sharp blade some four inches long.

McCall stamped heavily on Vara's hand, forcing him to give a cry of pain and let go of the knife; then he stooped quickly and picked it up. Vara got to his feet, holding his right hand with his left and cursing. McCall looked at the knife and then at Vara, shaking his head.

'You shouldn't do things like that, Eddie boy. You get all steamed up and you could do yourself an injury.'

Vara said nothing, but he was breathing hard. McCall tested the edge of the knife with the ball of his thumb. 'Sharp—real sharp. A man could shave himself with a knife as sharp as that.' He looked at Aston. 'I guess you wouldn't be wanting another close shave, would you?'

'No,' Aston said. 'One is enough.' That thin, deadly blade could so easily have been slipped in under his ribs if McCall had not thrust out a leg. He would need to watch Vara; the man was poison.

'You should take care what you say, Mark. Wise men don't go twisting a rattlesnake's tail. Get me?'

'I get you.'

'Give me my knife,' Vara said.

'You aiming to use it again?' McCall asked.

Vara did not answer.

'Give me your word you won't go sticking it into anyone in this hut and maybe I'll give it back.'

Vara still did not answer.

'So you don't really want it?' McCall made a move to put the knife in his pocket.

Vara said sullenly: 'All right. I give my word.'

'That's better,' McCall said. With a swift movement of his hand he threw the knife at Vara's feet. They were two inches apart, and the blade passed between them and stuck in the floor, quivering momentarily.

Vara had not moved. He bent down, gripped the handle and pulled the knife out of the floor.

*   *   *

They heard the sound only faintly at first, a kind of distant buzzing. It came nearer, growing louder, becoming unmistakable.

'Helicopter,' Albores said.

Aston began moving towards the door of the hut. Albores stopped him.

'Don't go outside.'

'You think it's looking for us?'

'It could be.'

Aston had not thought of that. It gave him a sick feeling to realise that there might even be eyes in the sky searching for them. This was what it was to be a hunted animal.

They all listened to the threshing of the helicopter as it came nearer. It was an ominous sound.

'Do you think they will search the mine?' Juanita asked.

'It is possible,' Albores said. 'We must hope they do not, but we cannot be certain.' He picked up one of the pistols.

Suddenly Vara cried: 'There it is.'

Aston looked out of the window and could see it. It was like a glass bubble with grotesquely large feet and a tail. It was so low he could see the two men who were sitting in the bubble. They could have been policemen.

'Keep away from the window,' Albores warned.

McCall and Vara moved to the table. Each

156

picked up a pistol and loaded it.

Aston thought for a moment that the helicopter was going to land; it hovered, almost touching the ground and raising small dust storms with its rotor blade. But the men in it must have been satisfied with just a look around, for very soon it lifted again and went clattering away like an ungainly bird. It was well that the Ford had been hidden; a car standing in the open would undoubtedly have aroused suspicion.

'Well,' McCall said, 'we know one thing now—they surely are searching.'

'And they could find us,' Juanita said. She seemed to be in low spirits.

Albores patted her shoulder. 'Don't worry. Tomorrow we shall be where they cannot touch us.'

'I think it's time I heard about that,' Aston said. 'You've never told me the escape plan.'

'No,' Albores said, 'we haven't, have we?'

'So don't you think it's time you did?'

'You still think we should take you along?'

'It's up to you. If you intend to throw me to the wolves, I can't stop you.'

'Perhaps you would be better with the wolves than where we're going.'

'Where are you going?'

'Well,' Albores said, 'I see no harm in telling you now. We are going to Cuba.'

When he came to think about it, he saw that it just about had to be Cuba. What other country in Latin America would have been so ready to give them sanctuary? But what would Cuba hold for him, even if he were allowed to stay? It was not a country to which he felt at all attracted, but what choice did he have? If the others were going to Cuba he must either go with them or stay where he was.

'I don't see you leaping with joy,' McCall said. 'Don't you like Castro's boys?'

'I've never met Castro's boys.'

'You do not wish to go to Cuba?' Albores asked.

'No,' Aston said, 'I don't want to go to Cuba, but even less do I wish to stay with the wolves. So, if I have the choice, I'll tag along. How do we get there?'

'Fishing-boat. It was been arranged.'

'I hope the arrangement works,' Aston said; but he was not counting on it. Things had a way of going wrong.

'It will work,' Vara said, 'if no one betrays us.'

It was not necessary to ask who he thought might do so.

'Before it gets dark,' Albores said, 'I think we should eat.' He opened the polythene bag and took out two loaves of bread and a slab of cheese. 'Simple fare, but it is not the most luxurious of hotels.'

They began to eat. Albores tried to pick up a news bulletin on the radio, but there seemed to be only pop music on the air and a lot of static. He switched off.

'We will try again later.'

Bread and cheese washed down with Coca-Cola was not the kind of meal Aston would have chosen, but he was hungry and accepted what was offered. In contrast, Juanita seemed to have little appetite; she drank some Coca-Cola but merely nibbled at the food. Albores tried to persuade her to eat more, but she shook her head.

'I am not hungry.'

'It could be some time before we get another meal.'

'It doesn't matter.'

Albores shrugged. 'As you wish.'

He switched on the transistor set again. There was still a lot of static and reception was poor, but after some juggling with the controls he succeeded in picking up a news bulletin from Radio Mendoza. As might have been expected, it was largely devoted to the celebrations of the Feast of the Scorpion and the visit of the American Vice-President.

'Large crowds watched the procession to the Plaza Lopez, and so great was the crush that at one point along the route the President's car was stopped for several minutes by a cheering mass of people who broke through the police and military cordon, completely blocking the Avenida Almirante Diaz. Order was soon restored and the procession continued on its way. Wreaths were laid on the monument to the great liberator, Pedro Lopez, and the people were addressed both by President Figueiras and by the Vice-President of our great northern ally, the United States of America.'

There followed lengthy summaries of both speeches, interspersed with recordings of what were apparently considered to be the highlights. There had been no mention of any assassination attempt.

'They are hushing it up, of course,' Albores said. 'It would damage the reputation of the Government if it were to be admitted that such a thing had happened.' He made a move to switch the set off. 'This stuff turns my stomach.'

'Wait,' Aston said. 'There may be something yet.' He wanted to know about the child.

Albores left the radio switched on, but he walked away and stared moodily out of the window. The news reader's voice continued its battle with the static.

It came almost at the end of the bulletin, an item apparently of low priority: 'A child, Anita Robles, aged ten and a half, was accidentally shot in the chest while watching the procession from the balcony of her father's apartment on the Avenida Almirante Diaz. She was taken to hospital and an operation has been performed to remove the bullet. She is reported to be dangerously ill. It is not clear precisely how the shooting occurred, but it is thought to have

160

been a ricochet. There is no suspicion of foul play.'

'How do you like that?' McCall said. 'No suspicion of foul play, hell! They must've found the rifle. They must've put two and two together. They know.'

'Of course they know,' Albores said, without turning. 'It's as I told you: they are hushing it up.'

There was one more item of news to interest them: 'A young police officer, José Martinez, was knocked down and killed by a hit-and-run driver in Pizzaro Road this afternoon. There were no witnesses, but it is believed that Officer Martinez had challenged the driver and was brutally run down. Police are searching for the car and the killer, and an arrest is expected very soon . . .'

'Ha!' Vara said. He reached across and switched off the radio. 'Ha!'

Albores said softly: 'It will need to be soon.'

CHAPTER TWELVE

GARCIA

It was not completely dark in the hut. The moon had risen and its cold silvery radiance came faintly through the window. The five temporary occupants were shadowy, indistinct

161

shapes that moved now and then, like people stirring in their sleep. But not one of them was sleeping.

A small red glow, brightening momentarily from time to time, served as a kind of beacon to mark where Albores was smoking. McCall sat with his hands in his pockets and his bony legs stretched out; Aston and the girl sat side by side on the bench, waiting for time to pass; Vara was standing, leaning against the wall, as though that were the most relaxation he would allow himself. No one was talking. Earlier there had been sudden spurts of conversation, much of it rancorous, but even the rancour seemed to have burned itself out, leaving only a brooding silence, broken occasionally by a cough, a sigh, a yawn, the scrape of a match, the shuffle of feet.

Aston looked at his watch. It was ten o'clock. He wondered how much longer it would be before Albores gave them the signal to make a move. An hour ago he had asked the question and had received nothing in reply but a non-committal: 'Not yet.' Since then he had sat staring blankly at the moonlight and thinking gloomily of the future. What the devil could he do in Cuba? Assuming that he was even allowed to stay there. Assuming also, and it was a large assumption, that they ever reached the island.

He thought of the girl who had been shot and prayed that she would not die. But he

162

knew that even that was a selfish prayer, since he was praying not so much for the child's life as for the weight of her death to be lifted from his conscience.

It was getting on for eleven when Albores stood up and said: 'Let's go.'

They left the hut with their packs slung on their shoulders. Albores had the torch; but in spite of clouds that had come up and obscured the moon there was still enough light to make the use of it unnecessary for the present. Each of them had one of the pistols. Aston was carrying a Colt in the right hand pocket of his gabardine windcheater; he could feel the weight of it on that side. There was a full magazine in the butt and Albores had shown him how to put a round into the breech; he had also pointed out the safety-catch. Aston hoped there would be no occasion to use the pistol, but Albores had persuaded him to take it. Albores could be very persuasive.

The air felt cool and there was a breeze blowing. It made an eerie whining sound. The girl shivered.

'You are cold, Juanita?'

'No,' she said. 'Not cold.'

'I thought you shivered.'

'It is nothing.'

Perhaps she had a sense of foreboding; that eerie whining of the wind could play on the nerves. It was playing on his.

They walked up through the gorge with

163

Albores in the lead, but when they got to the road they turned to the right, so that the sea lay ahead. They had been walking for about three-quarters of an hour when they came to the cottage, and they had met no one. Beyond the cottage were the dark shapes of other buildings, a small village, never a light showing; beyond that the glimmer of the sea.

A faint radiance was coming from a curtained window in the cottage and there was a pungent tarry odour that told of fishing gear.

Albores stopped, allowing the others to catch up with him. 'Wait here,' he whispered. 'I'll go and see if all's well.'

He walked forward and seemed to merge with the shadow of the building. A moment or two later a door was opened very cautiously and Albores was visible, framed in the doorway, with some other person beyond him only half seen. A few words apparently passed between the two, then Albores turned and beckoned with his hand.

'It's okay,' McCall whispered. 'Let's go.'

They moved towards the cottage. Albores had already gone inside, and the door was being held open by a swarthy, thick-set man dressed in patched trousers and a faded blue shirt. He looked about fifty, and his hair was thinning and turning grey; his face was as creased as an old suit and he had not shaved recently. He scrutinised them closely as they went in and seemed impatient to close the

164

door again, which he did immediately they were all inside.

There appeared to be only the one room, though part of it was screened off by blankets slung on cords, presumably to hide the bed and provide a little privacy. The floor was of earth, rammed down hard, with no covering, and the furnishing was Spartan—a plain deal table, a few wooden chairs, some shelves, an oil-stove, an oil-lamp hanging from a nail driven into a beam.

A woman was standing by the stove; she was probably about the same age as the man and she looked as worn as the dress she was wearing. It was easy to see that her life had been hard and unrewarding; she had an air of resignation, as though she knew there was nothing to hope for now and had accepted the fact.

Albores introduced them briefly: 'Pedro Garcia. Señora Garcia.'

The man inclined his head slightly, acknowledging the introduction. Aston thought he caught a gleam, a flicker of something in the hooded eyes; a kind of wolfish look. Garcia was not a man he would have trusted on sight, but no doubt he was being well paid for his services, and money could often command loyalty in the most unlikely of places.

'You will have some refreshment?' Garcia said. His voice was hoarse, as though he had

165

been doing a lot of shouting or smoked too much bad tobacco. 'A cup of coffee perhaps?'

Albores refused. He seemed ill at ease, which was unusual for him. 'I think we should go. There is no point in wasting time.'

'We must wait for Rodrigo.'

Albores looked at the man sharply. 'Isn't Rodrigo at the boat?'

'He is at the boat,' Garcia agreed. 'And he will come for us when it is time to go. When it is safe to go, you understand?'

'Why should it not be safe?'

'There has been much activity. The police—'

'The police have been here?'

'Not here, no. But they have been in the village. It is well to take precautions. So—we will wait for Rodrigo, eh?'

Albores sighed. 'If it must be.' He let his bag fall to the floor and the others set down their loads also.

'Now,' Garcia said, 'you will have some coffee? It is in the pot. Please sit down, señorita.' He drew up a chair for her. He was being hospitable, but to Aston it seemed that the hospitality had a certain spurious quality about it; he felt that it did not fit Garcia's character.

Since it was apparent that nothing more could be done until Rodrigo arrived, they accepted the offer of coffee. The woman put cups on the table, brought the pot from the stove and filled the cups. The coffee was

166

strong and black, slightly bitter on the tongue. The woman, having performed her task, retired again to her former position. She had not spoken a word; perhaps Garcia had trained her to be silent.

'There is one other matter,' Garcia said; and there was that wolfish look again. 'The question of money.'

'You have had the money,' Albores said sharply.

'I have had half the money. Now I would like the other half—if it is not too much to ask.'

'It is too much to ask. The agreement was that you should have the other half when we get to Cuba.'

'Perhaps it was,' Garcia admitted. 'And perhaps now I think it is too great a risk. Suppose when we get to Cuba you refuse to pay me. What then?' He rested his elbows on the table, staring across it at Albores.

'And suppose, if we pay you all the money now, you then fail to keep your side of the bargain. What then?'

Garcia gave the impression of a man who had been deeply insulted. 'You do not trust me?'

McCall said: 'Why should we trust you?'

'I am an honest man,' Garcia said.

'Who says so?'

'Who has ever said otherwise?'

'So we must trust you,' Albores said, 'but

167

you will not trust us?'

Garcia gave him a sly look from under his heavy eye-brows. 'It is you who need the boat. It is not I who have to get out of the country fast. People who need to do that must expect to pay their way.'

Aston wondered how much Garcia knew— and how much he had guessed. Enough to know that he held the whip-hand, certainly.

'We have paid,' Albores said.

'But only half, señor. I must have the other half. I must have it now.'

There was a kind of suppressed eagerness about him, as though he could hardly wait to get his hands on the money. Aston wondered why. Was it simply, as he had said, that he did not trust them to pay him the second half of the fee when they reached Cuba or was there more to it than that? There was a smell about Garcia, a smell of stale sweat and bad breath; but there was another kind of smell also—the smell of deceit.

'We could take back what we have already paid you,' Albores said. 'We could go elsewhere.'

Garcia laughed softly. 'It is late for that, señor.' He might not know all the details, but he knew they needed him, knew that he had them in the hollow of his hand; and no doubt it pleased him that it should be so. 'Oh, yes, señor, it is very late for that.' There was a note of gloating in his voice, of triumph even, as though in a contest of wits he had come out the winner.

'And it is late to alter the terms,' Vara said in a low, hard voice. He was standing, and the knife was in his hand. He stood over Garcia and touched the fisherman's neck with the point of the blade.

Garcia showed no sign of fear; he merely laughed again; and when he spoke it was not to Vara but to Albores.

'You are an intelligent man, señor. Tell him how foolish it is to threaten me. You need me. If my throat is slit, what use am I to you?'

'He is right, Eduardo,' Albores said. 'The knife will not help.'

Vara hesitated; he seemed reluctant to take the knife away from Garcia's throat. He was so angry that it would not have surprised Aston if he had thrust it home, and to the devil with the consequences. Finally, however, he let it fall to his side and walked away from Garcia. But he kept it in his hand, perhaps as a warning that he might change his mind.

McCall suddenly got up from his chair, walked to the door and lifted the latch.

'Where are you going?' Garcia demanded.

'Outside,' McCall said. 'The air in here doesn't agree with me.'

'You should stay here. It would be safer.'

'You think it would not be safe outside?'

'That is possible.'

'I'll take the chance,' McCall said. He

opened the door and stepped out into the night.

'He should not have done that,' Garcia said, and he seemed to be uneasy. 'He should have stayed here.'

'He can look after himself,' Albores said.

'Perhaps. But we should have kept together.'

To Aston it seemed that Garcia was making rather more of the incident than it warranted. If McCall wished to take a breath of fresh air it was scarcely a matter to make a fuss about.

Garcia himself appeared to come to that conclusion after a minute or so, and he returned to the subject that was evidently uppermost in his mind.

'You will give me the money now, señor?'

Albores did not answer immediately, but Vara said: 'Give the old goat nothing.'

Garcia shrugged. 'If you do not wish to go to Cuba—'

'It is time Rodrigo came,' Albores said. 'What is keeping him?'

'He will come,' Garcia said. 'In time.'

'We should be on our way.'

'The money then. Perhaps when I have the money it will be time to go.'

He was stalling. Perhaps the story of waiting for Rodrigo to give the all-clear had been no more than a ruse to hold them until he could squeeze out of them the second half of the fee. Albores stared at him for a while and came to a decision. He must have realised that there was really no alternative.

'Very well; have it as you wish. But remember this—any double-dealing on your part could be very unhealthy. You might not live to enjoy the money.'

'There will be no double-dealing,' Garcia protested. 'I only wish to be sure that I am paid in full. I am not a rich man and I cannot afford to take chances.'

Albores dug into an inside pocket and drew out a fat manila envelope. He laid the envelope on the table between himself and Garcia. Garcia could not conceal the eagerness with which he shot out a hand and snatched it up. 'You will not object if I count it?'

'I should have been amazed if you had not,' Albores said.

Vara slapped his left hand with the blade of the knife, scarcely able to contain his anger. The woman still had not spoken; she was staring at the envelope as though mesmerised. Garcia tore it open with his thick, blunt fingers and pulled out the wad of paper money that was inside. He let the envelope fall to the floor and began to count the notes on the table, carefully and slowly, muttering the amount as he counted.

'Well?' Albores said when Garcia had finished. 'Are you satisfied now?'

'I am satisfied,' Garcia said. He stuffed the money in his pocket and stood up.

It was good timing. The door opened and McCall came in, followed by a lean young man with a black moustache and brass rings in his ears which gave him a gypsy look—or possibly the look of one of those old-time buccaneers who had sailed the Caribbean three centuries ago.

'Ah, Rodrigo,' Garcia said, 'we have been waiting for you. Is all well?'

'All is well. The police have gone.' The young man had a low, pleasant voice, and he smiled as he spoke. He was handsome, and the smile seemed to come easily. Perhaps a shade too easily.

'Then we will go,' Garcia said.

*   *   *

It was lying alongside a stone quay in a small natural harbour round which the village had grown. There were some other boats too, but no sign of life anywhere; at that hour it was apparent that everyone slept. It was a wooden boat, about fifty feet long and broad in the beam; probably old; probably—if the light had been good enough to observe such things—it would have been seen to be in need of a coat of paint and possibly some repairs here and there. This was immaterial if the craft was seaworthy.

A small rectangular structure near the after end, scarcely bigger than a sentry box, was probably the wheel-house, and slightly forward of this was an accommodation hatch leading to a cramped cabin with a settee on each side and table at the far end. There was also a paraffin cooking stove, and the cabin reeked of fish, stale fat and strong tobacco. Rodrigo led the way down and lit an oil lamp hanging in gimbles before going back on deck to help Garcia cast off.

They dumped their kit and heard Garcia shout something to Rodrigo in a hoarse voice. The boat rocked slightly.

'Well,' Albores said, 'it looks as if we shall soon be on our way.' He sounded relieved.

'I still don't think you should have given that old devil the money,' Vara said. 'It was not the way it was agreed.'

'It was the only way of moving him.'

'It was wrong, nevertheless,' Vara said.

Aston went up on deck. The stern of the boat had already swung away from the quay and Rodrigo was just letting go for'ard. He dropped the rope on to the deck and jumped down after it, landing catlike in the semi-darkness. The propeller churned water and the boat pulled away from the quay, then began to move towards the harbour mouth. A minute later they were clear of the land and heading out to sea.

Rodrigo came up to Aston, walking the boards with that catlike tread.

'You are happy now, señor?'

173

Aston could not see the smile, but he knew that it was there. There was a hint of amusement in Rodrigo's voice, possibly of mockery.

'It is a long way to Cuba,' Aston said. 'We are not there yet. It is early to be happy.'

'True. It is a very long way and the sea can be treacherous. You have been in Cuba, señor?'

'Never.'

'Ah.' Rodrigo seemed to think about that for a moment or two. Then he said: ' Perhaps you will like it there. And again, perhaps you will not.'

'I must take the chance of that.'

'Yes, you must take the chance.'

The engine of the boat was making a thumping sound; the deck had begun to lift a little, and there was a swish of water rushing past the bows. A light rain was falling, putting a slippery film of moisture on the boards.

Aston had the impression that Rodrigo was secretly laughing at him. He wondered why.

CHAPTER THIRTEEN

CHANGE OF COURSE

Garcia came down the steps into the cabin. He had apparently left Rodrigo at the wheel. He

174

stood at the foot of the companion-way, stroking his chin and looking at them with a contemplative expression on his creased face.

'You are comfortable in here?'

'Comfortable enough,' Albores said. 'We were not expecting luxury.'

'That is well. You would not find it in this boat. Carrying passengers is not our regular trade, you understand.'

'We understand.'

Garcia continued to stroke his chin and stare at them with a certain speculation. Aston wondered what was on his mind, but it was not long before Garcia himself provided the answer.

'You are armed, I think.'

He must have noticed the bulges of the guns in their pockets and did not need to be told what they were.

'One takes precautions,' Albores said.

Garcia nodded. 'Naturally. But there is no longer any need for precautions.'

'Are you suggesting that we should now throw our guns away?'

'I am suggesting that it might not be wise to take them into Cuba. If you like to give them to me, I will stow them in a safe place.'

McCall laughed. 'You think we'd give our guns to you? We would be really be in your hands then.'

'So you still do not trust me?'

'That's right. We still do not trust you.'

Garcia shrugged. 'As you please.' He did not seem disappointed. He had probably not really expected to get the guns from them. But Aston wondered why he should have tried. What interest did he have in the guns? It was certainly not going to worry him if they had trouble in Cuba. So perhaps he just wished to get his hands on the weapons so that he could sell them later; for if there was one thing Garcia could be trusted to do, it was to keep an eye open for the chance of a quick profit.

'You should try to get some sleep,' he said. 'I am sorry there are no beds, but that is how it is.'

'We shall do well enough without beds,' Albores said.

Garcia gave a nod and went away.

'There is treachery in that man,' Vara said. 'I can see it in his eyes.'

Aston was inclined to agree. Yet if Garcia had wished to betray them he could already have done so. The police had been in the village but he had not alerted them. So, despite his unprepossessing appearance, perhaps he was nevertheless trustworthy and could be relied on to carry out his side of the bargain. After all, were they not on the way to Cuba?

Albores put forward the same argument, but Vara was not convinced. He went up on deck and came back a little later, damp and morose.

'Find anything up there?' McCall asked.

Vara sat down. 'What would you expect me to find?'

'Which way we're heading maybe.'

'With cloud covering the stars? I am not a magician.'

'I can tell you the answer to that,' Albores said. 'And I do not have to go out on deck.' He searched in his pocket and drew out a small compass. He held it in the palm of his hand and waited for the needle to come to rest. 'North-north-east. On that course we should eventually come to Cuba, I think.'

Even Vara had to admit that this was so.

Albores put the compass on the table. 'I will leave it there so that anyone who wishes to do so can make a check. But now I think it would not be a bad idea to do as Garcia suggested and get some sleep. I for one am tired.'

Aston saw that Juanita was already dozing. McCall also closed his eyes and in a moment was gently snoring. The engine of the boat had got into a kind of rhythm and there was just enough motion to have a lulling effect. Aston leaned back and soon his chin was on his chest and he too was asleep.

*   *   *

He was not sure what had awakened him. There was still the same yellow light coming from the lamp, the same odour of fish and

177

rancid fat and tobacco, the same beat of the engine and slight roll of the boat. Nothing had changed—or so it seemed. And yet he had a vague feeling that something had. He sat there for a moment, trying to get the sleep out of his head; his mouth felt dry, as though full of old cobwebs, and he wanted a drink. He stood up; there ought to be some drinking water somewhere.

He put a hand on the table to steady himself and glanced down at the compass; and he knew then what was wrong. The compass needle, which had been pointing more or less towards the bows, was now pointing directly at the starboard side of the cabin. The boat had altered course by more than ninety degrees and was heading in a westerly direction.

He woke Albores and showed him the compass. 'It seems we are no longer making for Cuba.'

Albores was wide awake in a moment. He picked the compass up to make sure the needle had not stuck, but it still pointed the same way.

'Wake the others.'

Aston roused Juanita and McCall while Albores shook Vara into wakefulness. He showed them the compass.

Vara swore. 'I knew it. I knew there was treachery in that man.'

'I suppose he could be avoiding a reef or something,' the girl said; but she did not sound as though she believed it herself.

'No wonder he wanted our guns,' McCall said. 'The goddamn son-of-a-bitch.'

They were all remembering the way Garcia had tried to persuade them to hand over the guns, and the whole thing reeked of treachery. Aston looked at his watch; they had not yet been an hour at sea; it was probably the alteration of course that had awakened him.

Albores put the compass in his pocket. 'We will go and see about this.'

He started to move towards the companion-way but had taken no more than a pace when someone stepped down into the cabin. It was Rodrigo.

'Stop there!' Rodrigo said. 'All of you stop just where you are.'

They stopped where they were. Rodrigo was carrying a sub-machine-gun; it looked like on old Sten and he had probably got it for a song, or he might have stolen it. It made little difference how he had come by it as long as it worked. And even though it was rusty, it probably did that too.

'So it is a double-cross,' Albores said.

Rodrigo was smiling. 'Pedro and I have decided that it would be unwise and unpatriotic to help criminals escape from justice. We are law-abiding citizens.'

'Like hell,' McCall said.

'What are you proposing to do?' Albores said. He sounded calm.

179

'We are proposing,' Rodrigo said, 'to take you to Mendoza and hand you over to the authorities there.'

'Where you will expect to get a reward, of course.'

'That remains to be seen. If there is a reward we shall not refuse it. Poor men cannot afford to refuse anything.'

'You have taken our money.'

Rodrigo was still smiling. He had a lot to smile about. 'Of what use would it be to you in prison?'

It was all becoming clear now; although Garcia had not betrayed them to the police at the village, it was merely so that he could carry them to Mendoza in the hope of a reward for his zeal. And he would probably get one. He was on a winner all ways: he had got the passage money, he stood a good chance of netting a reward, and he would not even have the expense and trouble of a voyage to Cuba.

'Now,' Rodrigo said, 'I will have your guns. One at a time, and be very careful please, because I do not wish to shoot you but I shall certainly do so if anyone makes a false move.'

There was no reason to doubt his word on that score. The smile meant nothing when it came to the crunch. It was Hamlet who had spoken of a 'smiling, damned villain.' And, by heaven, he might have been talking about Rodrigo; the description fitted him like a well-made suit.

180

'You first, Señor Albores,' Rodrigo said. 'Take it carefully out of your pocket and do not point it in this direction, because that would make me nervous.'

Albores reached into his pocket and pulled out the Luger that was in it. And he took care not to point it in Rodrigo's direction.

'Now put it on the table,' Rodrigo said.

Albores did that too.

Rodrigo turned his attention to Vara and told him to carry out the same procedure. It was obvious that Vara would dearly have loved to disobey, but it was obvious also that he was not going to argue with the Sten. He put his Colt on the table. McCall was next; he also had a Colt. Juanita had the other Luger; she put it on the table with the other pistols. That left Aston, and he had no intention of doing anything stupid; he pulled the Colt from his pocket and placed it carefully on the table.

'Now, señorita,' Rodrigo said, 'you will please be good enough to empty one of the bags and put the guns in it.'

She hesitated momentarily and Rodrigo made a threatening gesture with the Sten.

'Do as he tells you,' Albores said. 'It would not help to have him shoot you.'

The smile was like a fixture on Rodrigo's face. 'There speaks a sensible man.'

Juanita unfastened one of the duffle-bags, tipped its contents out on the settee and put the guns inside it. 'Give me the bag,' Rodrigo said.

She handed it to him and returned to her seat.

Rodrigo held the bag in his left hand, but he was still gripping the Sten in his right, and his finger was on the trigger. He was wary and there was no chance of rushing him.

'I shall put these weapons in a safe place,' he said. 'It will be necessary, I fear, to keep you in here for the rest of the voyage. But it will not be long; it is not far to Mendoza and that will be the end of the trip.'

He backed towards the companion-way, keeping his eyes on them, not turning away. He reached the bottom step and felt for it with his heel. He got one foot on it and was lifting the other when the stern of the boat rose a little. It was not much, but it was enough to throw him off balance. He lurched forward, dropped the duffle-bag and made a grab at the rail with his left hand. For a moment his vigilance wavered, and in that moment something went hissing through the air, gleaming dully in the yellow lamplight. There was a faint thud, and Aston saw the handle of Vara's knife protruding from Rodrigo's chest. Rodrigo was not smiling any more.

McCall and Albores rushed at him, but McCall was a foot ahead. The Sten was sagging in Rodrigo's hand, but somehow, with a final, instinctive reaction, he brought the gun up and pressed the trigger.

In the confined space of the cabin the sudden chatter of the gun was startlingly loud. McCall fell instantly without a cry. Albores gave a kind of grunt and staggered to the settee on the port side. He sat down abruptly, clutching himself with both hands and gasping. Although he had been behind McCall one of the bullets must have passed through the American with enough impetus left to wound him also.

But there was no more firing. Rodrigo had fallen forward across McCall's dead body and was dead too. He was never going to profit from his treachery.

Then Vara seemed to go mad. With a kind of animal snarl he picked up the Sten gun and ran from the cabin. Aston, with a sudden presentiment of what he intended doing, shouted to him to come back. Vara might have been deaf for all the attention he paid. Aston stepped over the blood-stained bodies of McCall and Rodrigo and stumbled up the companion-way, hoping that he might yet be able to prevent Vara from committing the ultimate act of madness. But it was too late: even as he felt the cool rain on his face he heard again the chatter of the Sten, not so loud this time but quite as deadly; just the one burst and then silence.

He felt the boat heel over, as though the wheel had been given a turn, and he knew that Garcia also was dead. He hoped Vara knew something about navigation, because there was a lot of Caribbean lying between them and the coast of Cuba, a hell of a lot. All they needed now was a hurricane.

He went back into the cabin, for he felt no desire to see what Vara had done. Albores was lying on the settee with a cushion under his head. He appeared to have been shot in the left side just above the hip. Juanita had pulled up his shirt and was pressing a pad of cloth to the wound, but there was a lot of blood.

'So you were too late,' Albores said. He looked sick.

'Yes,' Aston said.

'He had shot Garcia?'

'I didn't look. I heard the gun.'

'It was a foolish thing to do.'

Aston heard the engine stop. A few minutes later Vara came down the companion-way. He was no longer carrying the Sten gun. He seemed calm.

'We have to decide what to do,' he said. 'I have stopped the boat and now we must think what action to take.'

'You have already taken the wrong action,' Albores told him. He did not sound angry, merely sad. A little weary also.

'In killing Garcia? Perhaps. But he deserved to die. I do not regret what I did.'

'Without Garcia,' Aston said, 'how do we get to Cuba?'

'That is the question we must discuss,' Vara

said. There was something almost unnatural about the icy calm that had come over him after the frenzy of a few minutes before. 'But first I think it would be well to move these bodies. Perhaps, Mark, you will help me carry them up to the deck.'

It was a distasteful but necessary task; the bodies could not be left where they were.

'Very well,' Aston said.

When they rolled Rodrigo over on to his back the knife was seen to be still protruding from his chest. Vara pulled it out and it seemed to resist the pull, as though the dead man were reluctant to let it go. Vara wiped the blade on Rodrigo's shirt and slipped the knife back into the sheath that was concealed inside the hip pocket of his trousers. Then he put his hands under Rodrigo's armpits and, with Aston taking the legs, carried the dead man up the companion-way. They laid him on the wet deck and went back for McCall. The rain was still falling and the boat heaved gently, making no headway, drifting at the whim of any current, any tide that might exert a force upon it. The darkness had moved in close like a grasping hand.

By the time they had finished their task the girl had tied a bandage round Albores's waist to hold the pad in place over the wound. Already the dark stain of blood was showing through. Albores's face was the colour of putty and he seemed to breathe with difficulty and some pain. He asked for a cigarette. Juanita lit one and gave it to him.

'Now,' Vara said, 'we must decide.'

Albores lay back with his head on the cushion. He drew smoke from the cigarette and allowed it to drift upward from his mouth.

'We cannot go to Cuba now.'

Vara nodded. 'I think that is so.'

'Without Garcia,' the girl said, 'we could never do it.'

'Even with Garcia I think it would have been impossible. I do not say this to excuse what I did. I need no excuse. But I think perhaps even Garcia could not have taken this boat to Cuba.'

'Why do you say that?' the girl asked.

'He intended only to go to Mendoza—a few kilometres. Would he have taken on sufficient fuel for a voyage to Cuba, a distance of possibly seven hundred kilometres?'

They all thought about it, and nobody seemed willing to make a bet that Garcia had done so.

'Suppose,' Vara said, 'we were to try to take this boat to Cuba, it could be we would find ourselves in the middle of the Caribbean with no more fuel and very little food or water. Personally, I would not wish to take that risk.'

'What do you propose?' the girl asked.

'To go back,' Vara said.

She stared at him. 'You propose to take this boat back to where we came from?'

Vara shook his head. 'Not this boat; it would be far too conspicuous. But there is a smaller one—a dinghy—which we could row. We cannot have come far. I think we could be ashore before daybreak.'

'And then?'

'And then we could go back to the mine and work out some other way of escape.'

'It is an idea,' Albores said.

'It is a greater risk than going on,' the girl said.

'I do not think so. We are none of us sailors, and even with enough fuel I would not give much for our chances of reaching Cuba.'

She looked at the bloodstained bandage on his wound. 'It will not be easy for you in a small boat.'

'I shall survive,' Albores said.

*   *   *

Vara took the money from Garcia's pocket before they left; it was not going to be any use to him. The dinghy was lying, keel uppermost, at the after end of the deck. They righted it and lowered it over the side. The rain had eased and the moon was showing through breaks in the cloud. They secured the dinghy by its painter and lowered the duffle-bags into it.

When they had done this Aston and Vara went back to the cabin and helped Albores up to the deck. His wound was paining him but he was able to walk with some assistance. Juanita climbed down into the dinghy and between them they managed to get Albores into it.

There was one task left to do. Aston and Vara returned to the cabin and Vara emptied the paraffin out of the stove on to the settees. Aston took the lamp from its bracket and both men retreated to the companion-way. Aston threw the lamp on to the starboard settee and thought for a moment that it had gone out; but then there was a muffled roar as the paraffin caught fire, and flames began to race along the settee. He turned and followed Vara on to the deck.

Albores was half lying at the bottom of the dinghy with his back propped against the stern and Juanita had unlashed the oars. Aston and Vara climbed over the gunwale of the fishing-boat and dropped into the dinghy. Aston freed the painter and they pushed off with the girl at the tiller. Flames were already leaping up from the hatchway in the deck and providing a lurid illumination. They took the oars and began to row. Astern of them the funeral pyre of McCall and Garcia and Rodrigo was burning fiercely.

Suddenly Vara swore. 'We forgot the guns.'

Aston was not sorry about that. He had seen enough of guns.

CHAPTER FOURTEEN

REFUGE

It was not yet daylight when they reached the beach. Aston's hands were blistered and his back felt as brittle as a matchstick. He guessed that Vara must be in much the same condition.

They lifted Albores out of the dinghy and carried him clear of the water. He could scarcely stand at first, but gradually strength seemed to come back into his legs.

'I am all right,' he said. 'I can walk.'

They unloaded the dinghy and then pushed it into deep water, hoping that the tide might float it away. Aston picked up Albores's pack as well as his own; and then, with Vara supporting him on one side and Juanita on the other, Albores began to walk with dragging steps. Aston followed them. He hoped they knew where they were going.

*　　　*　　　*

It was the first piece of really good fortune that had come to them since that moment when McCall had involuntarily shot an innocent child. By some combination of tide and current, by rough navigation with a pocket compass and much laborious rowing, they had

189

returned to a point on the coast no more than half a mile or so from the small fishing village from which they had started. When day broke they were already on the rough track down which they had come from the mine and it had started to rain again.

'It is not far now,' the girl said. She was trying to be cheerful, but Aston guessed that she was in reality in low spirits. He guessed that they all were. He knew that he himself was.

Albores's strength was going; his feet dragged more and more, and at every step he gasped with pain. Aston had taken over from Juanita, and he and Vara were almost carrying Albores. They struggled on in the ever-increasing rain with the injured man becoming a heavier and heavier burden.

They came to a stop. Albores seemed scarcely more than half conscious, and now that day had come there was the increasing danger that they might meet someone on the road.

'I think you should go on ahead and fetch the car, Eduardo,' Aston said. 'Enrique will never make it like this. We will wait for you over there.' He pointed to some stunted thorn bushes growing among the rocks on one side of the way. 'If you leave your pack here it shouldn't take you very long to get to the mine and back.'

Vara thought about it for a moment and

came to the conclusion that it was a sensible suggestion. Together they dragged Albores to the bushes and lowered him to the ground, placing one of the duffle-bags under his head. His eyes were closed and his breathing was laboured.

'Hurry, Eduardo,' the girl said.

Vara went off without another word, and he must have had some reserves of energy in his lithe, sinewy body, for he even managed to break into a trot. In less than a minute he was lost to sight in the falling rain.

Juanita looked down at Albores with a worried frown. 'He should have medical attention. A doctor.'

Albores must have heard. His eyes flickered open and he even managed the ghost of a smile. 'Don't worry,' he croaked. 'I shall be all right.'

Aston did not believe it. Albores looked a very sick man, a man who should have been in hospital. Even if they got him to the mine, what could they do for him?

'Listen!' Juanita said.

Aston listened, and he soon caught the sound that the girl had heard—a clicking of hoofs on the stony road. He peered through the thin screen of bushes and saw a man with two mules. It was difficult to tell for certain, but it looked very much like the man they had passed the previous day. This time, however, he was going in the opposite direction—

towards the village. He was wearing a battered felt hat, turned down all round, and had a piece of old canvas draped over his shoulders to shed the rain. He had a stick in his hand and he was walking on the near side of the mules with his shoulders hunched and his gaze directed at the ground in front of him. He had almost passed the bushes when he looked up and turned his head.

It was obvious that the screen had not been enough to hide them from his keen eyes, for he said something to the mules in a harsh voice and they came to a halt, waiting with patient resignation for further orders, the bulky panniers hanging on each side of them and water trickling down their legs. The man looked towards the bushes, standing motionless for a while; then he began to walk towards them, picking his way carefully over the rough ground.

Aston and Juanita, who had been crouching down, stood up and faced the man. Under the wet felt hat his face was deeply lined, darkened to the colour of old mahogany by exposure to the sun. He looked old, but his eyes were bright and intelligent. They were watchful too. He glanced down at Albores.

'There has been an accident?'

'A small accident,' Aston said.

'You need help perhaps?'

'Help is on the way.'

'So?' The man looked again at Albores. It

was impossible for him not to see the blood on Albores's clothes. 'He was in a fight?'

'No,' Aston said. 'I told you—it was an accident.'

The man's gaze moved over the surroundings—the bushes, the rocks, the nearby hills; and he was certainly thinking about that accident—and wondering.

'It was a knife, señor?'

'A knife?'

'He was using a knife and it slipped?'

'No, it was not that.'

There was silence except for the patter of the rain. Aston suspected that the man would have liked to ask bluntly what exactly the accident had been, but could not bring himself to do so. Aston did not help him.

Finally the man said: 'And you do not need help?'

'Help will come,' Aston said.

The man shrugged. He made a kind of bow to Juanita and walked away. He reached the mules and shouted at them as though in sudden anger: 'Hi-yah! Hi!' He flicked at the mules' rumps with the stick and they started on their way again. The man tramped along beside them, shoulders hunched, not looking back.

'That was unfortunate,' Aston said.

'You think he was suspicious?'

'Only a simpleton would not have been. And he was no simpleton. He saw the blood.'

'You think he will talk?'

'He will talk,' Aston said. 'You can be sure of that.'

They waited while the minutes passed, watching the road in impatient expectation—and also a little in fear.

'Perhaps the car is gone,' Juanita said.

'Who would have taken it?'

'I don't know.'

'It has only been there one night. It's unlikely that anyone will have found it.'

'Perhaps it will not start.'

'That is more likely,' Aston admitted.

But it came at last; and in fact Eduardo had been gone no more than twenty minutes. It had seemed longer.

He turned the car, got out and walked to the bushes.

'Is all well?'

'An old man with two mules stopped and spoke to us,' the girl said. 'He seemed inquisitive.'

'I passed him on my way to the mine. He did not speak to me.'

'I think he will talk,' Aston said. 'He saw that Enrique was injured. He asked about it.'

Vara cursed softly, 'Well, it cannot be helped. Let us get him to the car.'

They met no one on the way to the mine. Vara drove the car over the rough ground and the rusting rails into the cave-like entrance. It was like going into a railway tunnel, the dark walls and roof closing about them. Vara took the car in for about thirty yards and stopped.

'Wouldn't it have been better to take Enrique to the hut?' Aston asked.

'It will be safer here,' Vara said. 'And perhaps drier too. In a heavy rain I don't think the roof of that hut would be very effective.'

Albores was lying across the seat in the back of the car and Juanita was supporting his head. Vara switched on the interior light and Albores opened his eyes. He spoke in a weak voice.

'We are at the mine?'

'Yes,' Vara said.

'What do you plan to do now?'

Vara did not answer. With Albores in his present condition any hope of escaping over the border could be utterly ruled out. They could not travel in the car, for even if there had been passable roads the car would have been stopped for certain. To go on foot was also out of the question. So what alternative was there? To stay at the mine until Albores recovered? But was it likely that he would recover in such conditions?

It was an uneasy silence. The difficulties of the situation were too apparent to need any spelling out.

'We should perhaps have tried the other way after all,' Albores said musingly. 'But it is a little late to think of that now.'

Vara looked at him, his dark face hard and expressionless. Aston guessed what was passing in Vara's mind: he was thinking that without Albores it would have been easier to get away; Albores was undoubtedly the burden holding them all back. But Vara said nothing; it was the girl who spoke.

She said: 'I still think we should get you to a doctor or a hospital, Enrique. What can we hope to do for you here?'

Vara said quickly: 'If we take him to a doctor or a hospital we are finished.'

'You would prefer to let him die?'

'I did not say that.'

'Perhaps it is not necessary to say it. It could be true nevertheless.'

Vara glared at her in anger, but she stared back at him unflinchingly. It was a moment of tension which was broken by Albores.

'I shall not die.'

Coming from a man who looked as bad as he did, it seemed a pretty optimistic statement.

It was still raining. Aston walked to the entrance and looked out. The downpour had become so heavy that it was only just possible to make out the huts against the cliff. Vara had probably been right about the roof; it was hardly likely to be proof against a torrent such as this. Pools of water had formed and there was an eager gushing of newly-born rivulets; the air was warm and steamy, like a Turkish bath.

Aston thought about the mule-driver. Perhaps he had already told the police what he

196

had seen; perhaps even now a search of the area was being prepared. And if the police came to the mine they would be trapped; there would be little hope of escape. He thought of the kind of life he had led before getting caught up with Juanita and the others; it seemed like another existence, another world—peaceful and infinitely distant. If only he could go back to it, could wipe out the past few weeks; if only he could do that. Yet to do so would be to erase Juanita from his life, to banish all that he had shared with her, the desperate ecstasy of their brief time together. Even at such a price as he had paid, and was yet perhaps to pay, it had been worth while. And indeed it had been more than that: from the moment of their first meeting it had been inevitable.

He turned and went to join the others.

'Suppose the police come,' he said. 'We shall be trapped in here.'

'We should not have forgotten the guns,' Vara said. 'We should have brought that Sten.'

'Guns would not help us. If we had guns it would just mean more killing, and in the end the result would be the same.'

'They may not come,' the girl said. But she did not sound very hopeful.

Albores's eyes were closed; he was huddled on the back seat of the car in his wet clothes and was breathing noisily. That grey look was still on his face.

Vara switched off the interior light. 'There is no point in wasting the battery.'

Aston took the torch and went to explore the mine. The tunnel went into the hill, sloping gently downward. The sides and roof were shored up with timber, but in places the timbers had cracked under the strain. Here and there he came to a pile of fallen rock and earth which he had to climb over. After about a hundred yards the tunnel split into two branches. He took the left-hand branch and continued to follow it, probing deeper into the old workings.

The air had a dank, earthy smell, and he suddenly heard the sound of dripping water. He shone the torch on the roof and saw where the water was coming though a fissure in a steady stream. It had formed a pool on the floor and was flowing from the pool down the slope of the gallery, deeper into the mine. Even as he watched there was a harsh creaking sound, as though unbearable strain were being put upon the planking, and with startling suddenness a sludgy mass of earth and water cascaded from the roof like cement being tipped from a mixer. He jumped back just in time to avoid the fall and watched it piling up on the floor. It looked as though the torrential rain was seeping into the hill and finding its way through to the galleries of the old mine, and the thought came to him that he could easily be trapped by one of these falls of roof.

198

He decided to explore no further but to go back to the others.

'Did you have a pleasant walk?' Vara inquired with a faint sneer.

'I had a walk,' Aston said. 'I wouldn't say it was particularly pleasant. What did they get out of this mine when it was in use?'

'Silver.'

'And the silver ran out?'

'Presumably.'

Aston went to the car and looked at Albores. Albores was awake and in pain; it showed in his eyes, in the way he breathed. Aston wished he could have eased the suffering, but there was nothing to be done.

Juanita touched his arm and drew him away from the car so that Albores could not hear.

'Enrique is dying.'

'Surely it's not as bad as that,' Aston said. But he knew that it was.

'The bullet is still in him,' the girl said. 'He has lost a lot of blood and he is getting weaker. Without proper medical attention he will undoubtedly die. And proper medical attention does not mean lying on the back seat of a car in wet clothing.'

'But what can we do?'

'We could take him to Mendoza.'

'Eduardo would never agree to that.'

'Is it necessary to get Eduardo's agreement? You or I could drive the car.'

'That's true,' Aston admitted. But he was

thinking that it might be necessary to fight Vara first. And Vara still had the knife.

'We should think about it,' Juanita said. 'For Enrique's sake, we should certainly think about it.'

Vara had been searching in the boot of the car. He came over to them with two bottles of Coca-Cola.

'These were left. You would like a drink?'

'I am thirsty,' the girl confessed.

Albores appeared to have dozed off or to have lost consciousness. They decided not to try to rouse him but to leave some of the Coca-Cola so that he could have it if he awoke.

Aston tackled Vara on the other matter. 'Juanita and I think we should take Enrique to Mendoza so that his wound can be attended to.'

Vara's face hardened. 'You must be crazy.'

'He's dying,' the girl said. 'Do you want him to die?'

'I don't believe it,' Vara said. 'It is not a bad wound.'

'How do you know how bad it is?' Aston asked.

Vara tugged at the lobe of his ear. 'I think we should not be hasty about this. He is sleeping now; that will do him good. Perhaps we should all get some sleep.'

'And then?'

'And then we will see what is to be done.'

Aston turned to the girl. 'What do you

think?'

She seemed doubtful, but she glanced at Vara and perhaps she was thinking how difficult it would be to move him. The possibility of conflict between the two men might have occurred to her also. Whatever the reason, she finally agreed to do as Vara had suggested.

'We are all tired. And perhaps later it will have stopped raining.'

'One of us must stay awake,' Vara said. 'If you wish, I will do the first watch. Two hours? Does that suit you?'

'It suits me,' Aston said.

He got into the front seat of the car and he really was tired. In spite of everything he was asleep almost immediately, and scarcely a moment seemed to have passed before he was being roused by Vara. He could not believe that he had slept for two hours, but a glance at his watch proved that it was so.

'Nothing has happened,' Vara said. 'It is still raining.'

Aston got out of the car, feeling stiff and heavy-eyed, and Vara took his place beside the sleeping girl. He closed the door softly and walked to the opening and looked out. As Vara had said, it was still raining, and a small stream of water was flowing into the mine. It was no lighter; if anything, the clouds seemed to have thickened and there was never a glimpse of the sun. The monotonous sound of the rain served only to deepen the mood of depression that already possessed him. He could see no way out of the predicament they were in. Whether they took Albores to Mendoza or not, there would be no escape, he felt sure of that; escape was nothing but a dream in Vara's mind; a mirage drawing him on.

An hour passed, and he was having difficulty in keeping his eyes open when he heard the whining of a motor engine in low gear. Keeping back in the shadow of the tunnel, he peered out and saw a jeep grind to a halt in the open space between him and the huts under the cliff. The hood was up and he could not see the men inside, but he guessed that they were police, and he guessed also that the old mule-driver had been talking. They were probably searching all the likely hiding-places in the area.

The men in the jeep seemed to be in no hurry to get out, but Aston did not wait for them to make a move; he ran back to the car, wrenched open the door and roused Vara and the girl.

'It's the police. In a jeep.'

CHAPTER FIFTEEN

TUNNEL

There was only one way to go: deeper into the mine. The girl went on ahead with the torch while Aston and Vara followed, carrying Albores between them. Albores had not awakened; he seemed to be in a coma. They went at a slow trot, maintaining a footing with some difficulty on the wet and muddy floor, panting under the weight of their burden and expecting at any moment to hear sounds of pursuit.

Juanita came to the fork, hesitated only momentarily, and chose the left-hand gallery. Aston remembered the roof fall, but it was too late to call her back. With Albores seeming to grow heavier with each step they took, he and Vara followed the girl and the wavering light of the torch.

When they reached the point where the roof had given way Aston saw that there had been a much greater fall; there was a mound of rock and soil almost completely blocking the gallery. Only on the right was there still a narrow passage between it and the wall, and water was still pouring through the roof and washing away at the mound.

The girl came to a halt and said in a low

voice: 'We can go no further.'

The men stopped also, still holding Albores between them and breathing hard.

'Perhaps we should go back and try the other tunnel,' Juanita said.

But already it was too late for that. As they hesitated the sound of voices could be heard in the distance, echoing hollowly through the mine.

'They have found the car,' Vara said. 'We cannot go back. We must go on.'

'Through there?' The girl shone the beam of the torch into the passage between the mound and the wall, and she shuddered, as though suddenly cold.

'It is the only way,' Vara said. 'They are coming. Don't you hear them? Go on!'

She went on without another word and they followed, the mud coming over their ankles and holding stickily, so that it was difficult to drag one foot after the other. It was like wading through treacle. But they came to the other side of the roof fall and there the mud was thinner. There was, however, far more water; a small torrent was flowing down the gallery, gurgling noisily. The girl still went on ahead, splashing through the stream, as the gallery continued to slope downward and to curve away to the left.

Aston soon noticed that the water was getting deeper; it was up to his calves, but it was not flowing so rapidly. Suddenly the girl uttered a cry of dismay and sank in up to her waist, as though a pit had opened in her path.

Vara dropped Albores's legs and went forward to help Juanita. She had sunk deeper by the time he was able to reach out and grasp her hand, and it was only after a considerable struggle that he was able to draw her back to the shallower water. She was soaked to the armpits and was breathing hard, but she had had the good sense to keep a grip on the rubber-cased torch.

Aston was supporting the still unconscious Albores.

'Well,' he said, 'this looks like the end of the line.'

There was no longer any sound of pursuit; just the throaty gurgling of the water.

'So,' Vara said, 'we have two choices. We can go back and give ourselves up or wait here for them to come and fetch us.'

'They may not come as far as this,' Aston said. 'They may think no one would go past the roof fall. When they have searched the other gallery they may go away. After all, they don't know for certain that we're in the mine.'

'They'll have seen the car.'

'The car proves nothing. We could have abandoned it. When the old man saw us we were on foot, remember.'

They sat Albores down in the water with his back propped up by the wall of the gallery. Aston and Vara supported him, one on each side.

'Switch the light off,' Vara said. 'It could give us away.'

The girl did so and they were plunged immediately into impenetrable darkness. The water rippled past their legs, tugging at them as though with invisible fingers. Aston felt chilled. Something touched his arm; it was the girl's hand.

'I wanted to make sure you were there,' she whispered.

He understood. The darkness was so complete that nothing was visible; one could imagine oneself utterly alone. He had the feeling of being sealed inside a tomb and had an insane impulse to start running back along the tunnel, searching for daylight, for the open air.

Then they heard again the sound of voices; but not loud; a kind of distant murmur.

'They are at the roof fall,' Vara whispered.

A faint glimmer of diffused light shone on the curving side of the gallery, wavered a moment or two, then vanished. A second later the light appeared again, and Aston guessed that the men back there were trying to see beyond the roof fall, shining torches through the gap and possibly debating among themselves whether or not to go any farther.

The light faded again, and suddenly there was a rattle of gunfire, as though someone had loosed off a score or so of rounds with a sub-machine-gun. This was followed by a burst of laughter that came in eerie echoes down the tunnel. Aston felt the hand on his arm tremble, as though that eerie laughter had touched the girl's nerves, sending a thrill of terror through her body.

They waited, unspeaking and motionless; and once again there was only the low gurgling of the water to break the silence and no light in the enveloping darkness that had closed on them like a wall of pitch.

After a while Vara gave a long sigh. 'They are not coming.'

'So what do we do now?' Juanita asked.

'We wait. What else can we do?'

'And Enrique?'

'Enrique must take his chance.'

Aston bent down and listened for the sound of Albores's breathing. He thought he detected in it a change; it seemed more laboured and uneven; very rapid for a few moments like an engine racing, then slowing down again. He straightened up.

'I think that chance is getting slimmer.'

'Nevertheless, we must wait.' There was a steely quality in Vara's voice that did not invite argument.

They waited while an hour slowly passed. The water became gradually deeper and they moved farther up the gallery. They were wet, tired, hungry and depressed.

Aston said: 'I'll go and see whether they've

gone.'

Vara made no objection. He merely said: 'Be careful then. It may be a trap.'

'Someone must go sometime.'

'You will need the torch,' Juanita said.

It would mean leaving them without any means of breaking the oppressive darkness, but it was necessary.

'I will come back as soon as possible,' he said; and he took the torch from her hand.

There appeared to have been another fall of roof where the water was pouring through; he could only just squeeze a way through and he debated in his mind whether it might not be advisable to go back and bring the others beyond this point before going on, in case there should be yet another fall. But he decided to press on; it should not take him long to discover whether the police were still there, and as soon as he had done that he could hurry back. He was using the torch sparingly and keeping it pointed downward, and when he reached the fork he switched it off altogether, going on in darkness until he came to the first glimmer of light that told him he was drawing near the entrance to the mine.

He moved even more cautiously now, pausing from time to time and listening. He could hear no sound of voices and there were no flashes of light from torches. He came to the car, opened one of the doors noiselessly and peered inside. It was empty. He walked to

208

the entrance and saw that the rain was teeming down as hard as ever. He could see no jeep. He took a few steps out of the mine and looked all round, but there was no sign of it or of the men who had been in it. They had gone. They had probably been gone for an hour. That burst of sub-machine-gun fire had no doubt been the signal for departure, a kind of farewell gesture, a joke perhaps, derisive as the laughter that had followed it.

He turned and went back into the mine, switched on the torch and began to run. At the fork he branched off into the left-hand gallery and continued running. When he came to the roof fall he stopped; he had no choice but to do so, for there was no longer any way through.

Shining the beam of the torch on that pile of rock and earth, he could see no gap anywhere; it filled the gallery from one side to the other. Where there had been a narrow passage on the right through which it had been possible to squeeze a way, there was now an unbroken muddy wall. How far the blockage stretched down the gallery he could not tell; there might be yards of it if there had been a really big fall; to dig through such a barrier might take days rather than hours. The thought of Juanita trapped on the other side, trapped in that dark, flooded dungeon, almost sent him out of his mind. Albores and Vara were there too, but he gave scarcely a thought to them; it was the girl who filled his mind with dread.

He began to shout, then stopped and listened. He could detect no reply, no sound but the ominous trickle of water and the thudding of his own heart. He shouted again, listened again. Nothing.

Frenziedly he began to tear at the obstruction with his bare hands, but after a few minutes he realised the futility of what he was doing. He needed a shovel; a pickaxe too perhaps, but most certainly a shovel.

With the torch in his hand, its beam wavering from side to side, he ran back along the gallery, searching for any implement that the long-departed miners might have left behind them. He found nothing to serve his purpose.

In desperation he went to the car. Perhaps there was something in the tool kit; even a tyre lever would be better than nothing. He opened the boot and saw at once the very thing he had been looking for—a small shovel. Perhaps in such a country, with such deplorable roads, a shovel was part of the normal equipment of a car.

Not hesitating for a moment, he seized the shovel and ran back to the barrier. He propped the torch up on a piece of rock a few yards back so that its light shone on the mound and began to dig.

There were blisters still on his hands as a result of the night's rowing; they broke and bled as he wielded the shovel. He ignored them, ignored the pain, ignored the ache in his back. He was soon dripping with sweat; it ran down into his eyes, half blinding him. He went on with his task, thrusting the blade of the shovel into the wet earth and flinging it away behind him. He concentrated on the right-hand side where the original way through had been, acting on the assumption that this was where the thickness of the barrier might be at its smallest. The bigger rocks he hauled out with his hands, cursing them for hindering him.

After a time the shovel struck something that was not a rock yet did not yield; it was one of the timbers that had supported the roof. He dug above and beneath it, then laid down the shovel, gripped the board and tried to haul it out. At first he could scarcely shift it, but by alternately thrusting and tugging he managed to loosen it, and suddenly it came away so unexpectedly that he fell over on his back and was half buried by a pile of mud and rock that had been brought down by the pulling out of the board.

Having with some difficulty struggled free, he saw that much of his work had been undone by this new fall, and in a kind of anguished ferocity he again attacked it until the very impetuosity of his efforts exhausted him.

He stopped this furious digging and took a grip on himself. He was in the position of a

211

long distance runner who has set off at a sprint and burnt up his energies in the first few laps, and he saw that he would have to take it more steadily if he wished to succeed in breaking through the barrier. His throat was burning; with his cupped hand he scooped up some water from a muddy pool and drank it feverishly. Then, having slaked his thirst, he began again, working at a slower pace and with more care.

By propping lengths of broken timber against the side of the gallery and other pieces at right angles to them, he was able to make a triangular-shaped tunnel and prevent more rubble from falling into it; but the tunnel was only some three feet high and he was forced to work kneeling in the sludge that filtered between the supporting boards. Now and then he shouted and listened for an answer, but none came. He began to despair. Suppose the barrier were so wide that he had as yet scarcely begun to penetrate it. How long could he go on like this? How long could the two men and the girl survive on the other side?

It occurred to him that it might be better to take the car and drive to Mendoza for help, and for a few moments he seriously contemplated doing so; but then he thought of the time it would take and of the trapped girl, and he started digging again.

He was having difficulty now in disposing of the material that he dug from the tunnel, since he had burrowed too far to be able to throw it clear. He solved the problem by using his windcheater as a kind of sledge which he piled with rocks and earth and then hauled backwards out of the hole. It was a slow process, but he could think of nothing better. Muddy water dripped on him continuously as he worked; he was covered in slime from head to foot, and was in constant fear that the tunnel would collapse and bury him. When, for the first time, he looked at his watch he was amazed to see that it was already half-way through the afternoon. He had been working for more than four hours.

He felt a terrible weakness creeping over him. He had eaten nothing since the previous day and had had little sleep. He doubted whether he could go on much longer; but he went on.

There was another worry now: the light from the torch was getting dimmer as the batteries became exhausted. How much longer would they last? And if they failed, could he still go on?

He had given up shouting long ago; he needed all the breath he had. When he heard the tapping sound he did not immediately realise what it was. But the tapping continued in a kind of pattern—three taps, a pause, three more taps—and he knew that it could only be someone knocking on the side of the gallery. He picked up a piece of rock and gave three taps on the wall at his right. Almost at once the answer came back quite loudly. He gave three more taps and set to work again with increased vigour, heartened by the assurance that someone at least was alive on the other side of the barrier. He wondered why they had not tried tapping before. But perhaps they had, and he had been too busy with his digging to notice it. Oddly enough, the idea of communicating in that way—the traditional one in mine disasters—had not even occurred to him until that moment.

It was two hours later when he finally broke through to the other side, and by then there was only the faintest glimmer of light coming from the torch. It was so weak that he could not even see who was there; but he recognised Vara's voice.

'You have been a long time coming back,' Vara said; and he gave a crazy sort of laugh as if the ordeal had affected his mind and thrown him mentally off balance.

Aston was still lying in the tunnel with the shovel in his hands and he was interested in only one thing.

'Where's Juanita? Juanita—are you all right?'

'She won't answer you,' Vara said.

Aston felt sick. Had he done all this just for Vara? He hated Vara for being alive.

'Why won't she answer? She's not—' He could not bring himself to say the word.

214

'No,' Vara said, 'she's not dead. Not yet, anyway.'

'What do you mean—not yet?'

'She's unconscious. I think a rock must have fallen on her head. You'll have to help me with her.'

Aston wriggled backwards out of the tunnel, dragging the girl while Vara pushed from behind. When they were all clear of it Aston shone the failing torch on her face. There was a gash in her forehead and the face was smeared with blood and dirt. Her eyes were closed, but she was breathing.

He stood up. 'Where's Enrique?'

'We lost him,' Vara said.

Aston did not ask how they had lost Albores. He glanced towards the tunnel, but there was really no question of going back to search for the other man.

'He would have died anyway,' Vara said. 'He was booked for the long journey.'

It seemed a heartless thing to say, but perhaps it was true. With the torch still in his hand, Aston stooped and lifted the girl's shoulders.

'Help me, Eduardo.'

Vara took her legs. Together, stumbling like drunkards, they began to walk.

CHAPTER SIXTEEN

NIGHT DRIVE

They laid her on the back seat of the car where Albores had previously lain. Aston wiped some of the blood and dirt away from the gash in her forehead, and it looked bad. He took a shirt from his duffle-bag, tore it into strips and made a rough bandage for the wound.

Vara watched him. When he glanced up he caught an expression on Vara's face which puzzled him.

'What are you proposing to do now?' Vara asked.

Aston said: 'Isn't that obvious? We must take her to Mendoza. She could die.'

Vara nodded. 'Yes, she could die.'

'Let's go then.'

'Not so fast,' Vara said. 'We are not going to Mendoza. We are going to make for the border.'

'You're mad. That's out of the question now.'

'No,' Vara said, 'it is not out of the question.'

Aston moved a step or two away from the car. The interior light was on, but there was not much other light in the mine. The sound of rain still falling came like a dirge and it was

216

growing dark. Vara, too, had drawn away from the car; he was like a shadow and there was no definition to his face. Impossible now to see what kind of expression it was wearing. His voice was low, but there was the hint of a threat in it. 'I hope you are not going to be a fool, Mark.'

'You think I would be a fool to insist on going to Mendoza?'

'I am sure of it.'

Aston remembered the knife Vara carried. Vara was ruthless and hated him. It meant nothing that he had saved the man's life; Vara might hate him all the more for that, regarding it as a kind of humiliation. He would certainly not hesitate to use the knife in order to get his own way. Yet, for Juanita's sake, they had to go to Mendoza.

'I could take the car. You could do as you please. I wouldn't be stopping you.'

'I need the car,' Vara said. 'It's a long journey to the border.'

'Okay then,' Aston said. 'Maybe you're right at that. Maybe it would be foolish to go to Mendoza.'

He walked to the back of the car and opened the boot.

'What are you doing, Mark?' Vara sounded suspicious.

'I thought there might be some of that Coke left.'

'No. We drank it all.'

Aston was groping about in the boot. 'We may have overlooked a bottle.'

'I tell you we drank it all.' Vara was moving towards the back of the car now. He was certainly suspicious.

'You're wrong.' Aston said. 'I've found one.'

He had indeed found something, but it was not a bottle of Coca-Cola. His fingers closed on the handle of a monkey-wrench.

Vara had come to a stop a couple of yards away from Aston and slightly behind him. Aston decided to give him one last chance of relenting.

'I thought you'd want to help Juanita. I thought you loved her.'

Vara gave that half-crazy laugh again. 'What gave you that idea?'

'It just seemed like it. Maybe I was wrong.'

'Maybe you were. And again, maybe not so far wrong either. Maybe I did love her once—a long time ago.'

'Not so long,' Aston said.

'It seems long. It seems one hell of a long time since you walked in.' Vara had edged a fraction closer. His right hand was hidden behind his back. 'You know the only one I love now?'

'Tell me.'

'Myself. No one else.'

'So you're not an idealist any more?'

'Right, Mark. I thought about things back there, shut in that black hole. When you're

218

likely to be dead fairly soon you start thinking. I thought, what in hell have I been doing all these years, planning to make a better world? Who am I, for God's sake? San Paulo in a black skin?' Again that laugh. Crazy. Crazy as they came. 'From now on, Mark, I don't go around looking after the world any more; I look after myself. Me. Eduardo Vara.

'And that means not going to Mendoza?'

'That means not going to Mendoza.'

Aston struck at him with the monkey-wrench back-handed, aiming for the head. But Vara was too quick; he stepped aside. The wrench just touched his shoulder; he staggered a little but kept his feet; and his right hand came from behind his back with the knife in it.

'So that's your game, Mark. You want to die? You really want to die?'

Aston wondered whether Vara would throw the knife, as he had thrown it at Rodrigo; but he did not think so. Vara would wish to make sure, and you could never be sure with a throw; if you missed the target you had disarmed yourself and were at a disadvantage.

He did not answer the question. He watched Vara. He felt sick and weak, and the monkey-wrench hurt his blistered hand. Vara was probably stronger, because he had done no digging; he moved like a cat, lithe and pantherish; and like a cat perhaps he could see in the semi-darkness of the mine. Aston was not seeing at all well; Vara seemed to merge

219

into the shadow, to become a shadow himself. Aston blinked his eyes, striving to see. He had to watch Vara, watch the knife.

Vara came in suddenly, swiftly, his knife-arm moving like a striking snake. Aston swayed to the right—not fast enough, not far enough. The knife went through his shirt, biting into the flesh of his waist on the left side, slanting upward, touching the rib. Pain lanced through his body; Vara's head there in front of him, still shadowy, undefined, a kind of phantom; bitter sickness in his throat. He lifted the monkey-wrench in his right hand and brought it down with all his remaining strength. He felt the jarring shock of the impact flowing up his arm; and Vara was not there any more; no shadow, no phantom, nothing. Vara was lying on the ground and his legs were jerking, as though he were trying to push something away from him. But there was nothing to push, and he was not really trying to do anything. No one ever tried to do anything after his skull had been crushed by the heavy end of a steel monkey-wrench.

Aston leaned on the car and looked down at his side. The knife was not in him now; Vara had wrenched it out in falling. There was no knife, but there was a hole in his flesh and the blood was draining out of the hole. It was not paining him much; it was just numb. He was feeling sick again; his head swam and he thought he might faint, but he knew that that was one thing he must not do, because he had to drive a car to Mendoza.

He worked his way round to the side of the car on legs that felt as though they were likely to fold under him at any moment, and he saw that the girl was still lying on the back seat just as she had been before he had killed Vara. There was no reason why his killing Vara should have roused her; Vara had not made a sound in dying. And even if he had cried out with all the power of his lungs she would not have come out of her coma; she was too deeply unconscious for that.

The duffle-bag from which he had taken the shirt to bandage her head was lying on the floor. He rummaged in it and found a towel. He made a thick pad with the towel and pushed it in under his shirt to cover the wound, tucking it into the waistband of his trousers to hold it in place and buttoning the shirt again. He slammed the rear door and clawed his way along to the front. He opened the front door and dragged himself in behind the wheel.

For a few moments he just sat there, his hands on the wheel and his head bent forward and resting on them. He felt a strong inclination to stay there and drift off into sleep, but he fought against the urge and reached out with his right hand, searching for the ignition key. It was not there.

He felt beaten. If he could not even start the

car, how could he hope to reach Mendoza? But Vara had started it. Vara must, therefore, have the key. Having come to this conclusion, he opened the door of the car and slid out. A sensation of dizziness came over him and he had to support himself with a hand on the door until it had passed. Then he made his way to the place where Vara was lying.

He was thankful for the darkness; it prevented him from seeing the crushed head too clearly. When he had taken the monkey-wrench from the boot it had not been in his mind to kill Vara; he had intended doing no more than knocking him unconscious. It was the knife-thrust in his side that had goaded him into striking with such killing force.

'You shouldn't have stabbed me, Eduardo,' he whispered. 'You shouldn't have done that.'

There was no answer from Vara. Aston began to search his pockets. He found the key, but in getting to his feet he had another attack of giddiness and almost fell. But he fought against it and got back into the driving-seat.

The thought flashed into his mind that the police might have immobilised it, but the engine came to life with no more than a momentary hesitation. He allowed it to warm up, then switched the lights on and reversed out of the mine.

It was completely dark now and still raining heavily. He gave himself turning room, then changed to forward gear and brought the car

222

round to the track by which they had come to the mine. The big Ford had automatic transmission and he was thankful for that; he had enough problems to deal with in his present state without the added one of gear-changing on an unfamiliar car.

There was a small river flowing down through the gorge. He had the windscreen wipers going and the head-lamps cut a swathe of brilliance through the darkness. There was no sign of any police, and he could understand why they would not wish to hang around in a jeep in such a downpour; they were probably in some more comfort-able place after having convinced themselves that there were no fugitives from justice in the mine.

He reached the junction with the upper road and turned left, away from the village. The road had been bad enough before the rain; now it was far worse: the pot-holes were filled with water and the surface was a mixture of rocks and mud. He had to fight to hold the car on the track; the wheels kept spinning and sliding in the treacherous slime, threatening to throw it completely out of control. He had sudden glimpses of steep slopes falling away in front of him, of rock-piles looming out of nowhere; and it was not only the car he had to fight but his own weakness, the fits of dizziness, almost of black-out. The wound in his side was a dull ache, and the blood was coming through the towel and through his shirt, soaking into his trousers, running down his leg.

When they reached the Mendoza road he stopped the car, switched on the interior light and looked at the girl. Her face seemed chalk-white where he had wiped the mud away and her hair was matted above the bandage. Her mouth was slightly open, but he could not hear her breathing and her appearance scared him. But there was nothing he could do for her except to get her to Mendoza as quickly as possible.

He switched off the interior light and brought the car on to the Mendoza road.

*   *   *

There were lights on in Peters's house. Aston sat in the car and looked at the lights, and his head swam. He hardly knew how he had got there, but he had managed it somehow. He had come to Peters because Peters was a friend, and living as he did on this side of Mendoza, it had not been necessary to drive through the city to get to him.

The drive had been a nightmare nevertheless, even where the road was better. There had been more traffic then, and he had had to concentrate hard while his mind kept trying to slide away from him. It had been like something out of a crazy film, with hairbreadth escapes from collisions with other vehicles and drivers hooting at him in warning and in anger and everything seen through a kind of gauze curtain that made it blurred and unreal.

But he had made it; he was here; the journey was over and he could relax. His head sank forward on to the steering-wheel and sleep began to steal over him; blessed oblivion. He closed his eyes.

But then he opened them again. It was not quite finished yet. What in hell was he thinking about? He had to talk to Peters, had to tell him about Juanita, tell him to get a doctor, an ambulance. Tell him.

He opened the door and tried to get his left leg out of the car, and it refused to move; he had to shift it with his hands because it seemed dead. But he got it out and he got his right leg out too. And then he was sliding himself out of the car, and his head was whirling and he had to hold on with both hands, waiting for it to clear. When it had cleared a little he turned and headed across the pavement with the rain drenching him like a shower-bath and that dead left leg refusing to act as it should have done. And Christ, he thought, I mustn't fall now; I've got to hang on for a little longer, just a little longer.

There was a wrought-iron gate and the catch baffled him for a time. But he got it open at last and he decided to take the path at a run because maybe that way he would not fall on his face. But it did not work out and he found himself lying on the gravel with a pain in his side as though a chunk of flesh had been ripped away. He lay there for a while and the rain lashed at him. He raised his head and he could see the porch over Peters's door with a light in it. The light seemed to be sparkling, but that was probably the effect of the rain; he watched it and had the idea that it was beckoning him. He began to crawl forward, and when he reached the porch he pulled himself up and stood there swaying and trying to find the bell-push. It eluded him; he had to take several stabs at it before hitting the target, and then he heard the sound of the chimes inside the house and he leaned on the door-post and waited for Peters to come.

But it was not Peters; it was Eva. She was pretty blurred because of that damned gauze curtain again, but he could see that much. She looked at him and gave a kind of squeak and her eyes widened.

'It's all right,' he mumbled. He wanted to reassure her because he knew that he must be a shocking sight. There was all that mud for one thing, and there was the towel stuck inside his shirt and the blood coming through. He must look terrible. He felt terrible. 'Oh, God!' he said.

He caught a glimpse of Peters behind Eva, and he was damned glad Peters was there because he needed him. God, he certainly

226

needed him right now.

'What is it?' Peters said. 'What—' And then he saw what it was and he brushed past Eva and stared at Aston. 'What on earth,' he said, 'have you been up to?'

It was not really the time or the place to go into all that; it would have been too long a story.

'The car,' Aston said. 'Juanita. Out there.'

He gave a vague wave of the hand in the general direction of the mad, and the curtain came down thicker than ever, thicker and thicker. He had an impression of falling, but he was out before he reached the ground and had no feeling of the impact.

*   *   *

He was lying in bed when he came round and the sun was shining. It was a clean, pleasant room with built-in cupboards and everything as neat and tidy as could be. He had just worked out that it must be one of the bedrooms in Peters's house when the door opened and Peters himself came in.

'Well,' Peters said, 'I see you've waked up at last. How do you feel?'

'I've felt better.'

'That's natural. But Dr. Gallegos says the wound isn't serious. You lost a lot of blood but you'll be all right. He gave you a sedative. I expect that's why you slept so well.'

There was something about Peters that worried Aston. Peters would not look at him; whenever his eyes encountered Aston's they veered away as though embarrassed. It could have been because Peters knew what he had done, what kind of operation he had been mixed up in. Peters would not approve of that; he would be horrified by the idea of an employee of the Anglo Insurance Company being wanted by the Mendoza police. But Aston did not think it was that which was embarrassing him.

'Juanita,' he said. 'Is she—'

Peters took off his glasses and began polishing them on a handkerchief. He concentrated on this task, not looking at Aston.

'I'm sorry,' he said. 'We liked her, you know. Such a pity it should end like this. Eva is very upset about it.'

Aston lay back on the pillow and stared at the ceiling. It couldn't be. Not after all he had been through. Not after that. Life could not be so cruel. Yet he knew that life undoubtedly could.

'I really am sorry,' Peters said.

CHAPTER SEVENTEEN

IF IT RAINS FOR EVER

The suit was blindingly hot as Aston walked to the waiting airliner at Mendoza's Pedro Lopez Airport. He was going home, going back to England; but he felt no elation, no lift of the heart; only a kind of greyness inside him like the grey colour of a December sky.

He supposed he ought to be feeling happy, thankful that the wound in his side had healed and that he was a free man. There could be no doubt that to a certain extent he had the Anglo Insurance Company to thank for that. He was not sure of all the details of how it had been done, though he suspected Peters knew; but a lot of palms had certainly been liberally greased, a lot of strings well and truly pulled. It was one of the advantages of dealing with a corruptible police force that, even if you could not buy justice, you could, if you had the money, at least succeed in bending the law a little.

Even so, there might have been more trouble if President Carlos Figueiras and his government had not been so eager to hush things up. A public trial, in the course of which Aston might have revealed that there had in fact been a plot to assassinate the Vice-

President of the United States of America and that it had so nearly succeeded, would have been a severe embarrassment to all concerned; while to throw an English subject into gaol without a trial might have caused friction with the British Government. Therefore, since all the participants except Aston appeared to be dead, it must have seemed better to let him go than to draw attention to an affair which could only serve to discredit a regime which tried to give the impression that it had the whole-hearted support of the people.

'You will have to leave the country, of course,' Peters had told him. 'And I am afraid the Company can no longer employ you. I'm sorry, but there it is. It was very foolish of you to get yourself mixed up with that rabble.'

'It was not a rabble. You can't call three men and a girl a rabble.'

'No? Well, perhaps not. Nevertheless, it was unfortunate.'

'Perhaps.'

'It was the girl, of course, who entangled you. I quite understand that. Eva understands too. She says you were infatuated and I think she is right. The infatuation blinded you to the difference between right and wrong.'

'Oh, no,' Aston said, 'I could see the difference well enough. I could see it very clearly.'

'Is that so? Well, it just shows what a powerful hold she had on you.'

'Let's not talk about it, shall we?'

'Still hurts, does it? Ah well, you'll get over it. One always gets over that kind of thing. Time is a great healer.'

It was easy for him to say that, Aston thought; but what did he know about it? He had no idea.

'Incidentally,' Peters said, 'that little girl who was shot—Anita Robles, I think her name was—she'll be all right. The wound wasn't nearly as serious as they thought at first.'

'I'm glad,' Aston said. 'Yes, I'm certainly glad about that.'

*   *   *

He climbed the steps to the door of the airliner and the stewardess gave him one of those big welcoming smiles that were part of the package. He found his seat and sat down and stared morosely out of the window at the Pedro Lopez Airport buildings roasting in the sun. Well, it was goodbye to all that. He hoped Peters made the grade, got to be manager. Peters was not a bad sort and he deserved to land the top job. He probably would, because he would never do anything to blot his copybook, and he would go on working for the Company until he retired on a pension. For Mark Aston there would never be any pension, and not even a golden handshake either. He was departing under a cloud.

231

He heard somebody slip into the seat next to his, but he did not look round. He was in no mood to start up a conversation; he just wanted to sit there and let the gloom settle round him like a thick grey cloak.

And then he heard her voice: 'Aren't you even going to look at me, Mark?'

He turned then. There was a small scar on her forehead where the rock had gashed it but that was all. She was a shade pale, like someone who had recently been ill, but she was as lovely as ever. Lovelier even. His heart seemed to stop beating and then race like a clock that had slipped its cogs.

'Juanita!' Softly, in wonder, in joy.

'So you have not forgotten me?'

He stared at her in amazement, in disbelief. 'I thought you were dead. Peters told me—'

'They let him believe that too. The police came and took me away that night and let him think I had died. It might well have been true; I was almost dead. I recovered in a prison hospital. Not a pleasant place, I assure you.'

'And then they let you go?'

'On condition that I leave the country and never return.'

'But I don't understand. Why would they do that?'

She smiled. 'My family still has some influence. And even though I have disgraced them they feel a certain responsibility.'

'Your family?'

'Didn't I ever tell you? My father is Minister of the Interior and my Uncle Manuel is Attorney-General. It would have embarrassed them to have me languishing in gaol.'

Aston whistled softly. So that was her mysterious background. If Peters had known that he would not have worried for a moment. And how wrong he would have been. 'But what an amazing coincidence that you should be travelling on this plane.'

Her lips twitched. 'Coincidence?'

'Now don't tell me,' he said, 'you knew I would be on this flight.'

'I made inquiries.'

'And you wanted to come with me?'

'I love you, Mark,' she said. 'Didn't I ever tell you that either?'

'You know I have no job?'

'It doesn't bother me. Does it bother you?'

'No,' he said, 'it doesn't bother me either. Nothing bothers me now, nothing.'

'I am looking forward to seeing England.'

'It will be raining.'

She gave a little lift of the eyebrows. 'Why do you say that?'

'It always is when I go home.'

'I don't mind if it is raining,' she said. 'I don't mind if it rains for ever.'